FREEDOM DANCE

FREEDOM DANCE

by

Dallas L. Barnes

HERE'S LIFE PUBLISHERS
P.O. Box 1576, San Bernardino, CA 92402

FREEDOM DANCE
by Dallas L. Barnes

Published by
HERE'S LIFE PUBLISHERS, INC.
P.O. Box 1576
San Bernardino, CA 92402

HLP Product No. 951202

Library of Congress Cataloging-in-Publication Data
Barnes, Dallas L., 1941-
   Freedom dance.
   I. Title.
PS3552.A6738F7   1986   813'.52   85-27112
ISBN 089840-108-9

FOR MORE INFORMATION, WRITE:
L.I.F.E.—P.O. Box A399, Sydney South 2000, Australia
Campus Crusade for Christ of Canada—Box 300, Vancouver, B.C., V6C 2X3, Canada
Campus Crusade for Christ—103 Friar Street, Reading RG1 1EP, Berkshire, England
Lay Institute for Evangelism—P.O. Box 8786, Auckland 3, New Zealand
Great Commission Movement of Nigeria—P.O. Box 500, Jos, Plateau State Nigeria, West Africa
Life Ministry—P.O. Box/Bus 91015, Auckland Park 2006, Republic of South Africa
Campus Crusade for Christ International—Arrowhead Springs, San Bernardino, CA 92414 U.S.A.

This book is dedicated to the brave man
who may never read it — the one who returned.

Contents

"Where the Spirit of the Lord is, there is liberty."

2 Corinthians 3:17

1

The Russians Are Coming

THE WARM SEPTEMBER SUN climbed into the morning sky, filtering hazy light through a lingering smog that hung over Los Angeles like smoke over an ashtray. The freeways were nearing the critical peak as a seemingly endless flow of cars wound their way over the ribbons of concrete, bringing the morning rush hour once again to the brink of paralysis. Above it a collection of Cessnas and helicopters buzzed and hovered, filling the air with a mix of conflicting traffic reports for the all-important drive time. The banter between the morning DJs and their airborne eyes filled the AM dials with happy talk.

In the Valley it was 74 degrees after an overnight low of 68 at the civic center. The beach, stretching along the coastline like a gray sandy rope from San Clemente to Malibu, was already beginning to draw its daily collection of sun worshippers. The crowds were smaller now; the official end of summer on Labor Day and the beginning of a new school year had taken away many of the brawny young. But there were still California's ageless — those who arrived in Porsches, those with tanned, oiled, glistening, wrinkle-free bodies and blonde hair, those who look very much like Ken and Barbie.

On Barham Boulevard employees of Warner Studios were

already near the middle of their work day with a collection of new features whose crews had been shooting since dawn's first light. Only a few miles away the sprawling Universal Studio was busy with the production of six television series.

Downtown, truck after truck brought tons of fresh vegetables and citrus to the inner city's produce market, where the air hung sweet with the aroma of ripening oranges. In San Pedro Harbor a line of supertankers stretched seaward, awaiting a turn to pump their syrupy black crude into the refineries dotting the Southbay curve.

Along Wilshire Boulevard the telephone lines hummed with voices and the electronic code of computers as man and machine alike linked themselves with the Blue Chip markets in the East. In Hollywood an army of agents worked on deals while at the Los Angeles Street bus station Greyhound after Greyhound brought more would-be starlets.

The jet set, trend-setting, fashionable Los Angeles was beginning another day. And in the midst of this collection of asphalt, palm trees, suntan oil, sports cars and capitalistic glitter were one hundred sixty-seven citizens of the Union of Soviet Socialist Republics. Russians.

These Russians, spread over the three upper floors of the University Hilton on West Jefferson Boulevard in South Los Angeles, were not typical Soviet citizens. Typical Soviet citizens did not travel abroad. One hundred twenty-five of these Russians were the pride of the motherland. They were showcased to the world as the Supreme Soviets. They were the beautiful people of Russia — the elite, hand-picked, carefully trained, impeccably groomed, world-renowned Bolshoi Ballet troupe.

In the Soviet Union the members of the Bolshoi troupe lived as aristocrats. Many had apartments in central Moscow, private automobiles, western clothes, and privileges the average Russian did not dare dream of. Beyond the borders of the sprawling Motherland the members of the Bolshoi took on legendary characteristics. They were known for their dedication, discipline, and perhaps most important, their excellence. To the world of classic dance the Bolshoi was the standard by which all others were measured. And as such, the leaders of the Kremlin were quick to identify themselves and their government with the Bolshoi. After all, wasn't the excellence of the Bolshoi simply a reflection of the Soviet doctrine? Didn't the fact that many of the trainers, managers and dancers were members of the Communist party prove it? The Kremlin thought so, and thus, the Bolshoi, basking in the warm atmosphere of détente, had been sent to the United States for a three-month tour.

Three major cities were chosen by the publicity-conscious Russians—New York, Chicago, and Los Angeles.

It was Friday, September 14, 1979, and the Bolshoi Ballet had three performances remaining at the Los Angeles Shrine Auditorium. The finale was scheduled for Sunday night. Yuri Grigorovich, the troupe's artistic director, had selected *Swan Lake* for the crowning final performance of the three-month tour. He was certain the applause would echo in the ears of the world of dance until the Bolshoi returned again. Yuri Grigorovich was closer to the truth than he dared think. The Bolshoi's final performance in Los Angeles was going to be one that the world of dance would never forget, and neither would the Kremlin.

After the performance there would be doubt that the troupe would ever return to the United States. There was no doubt that Yuri Grigorovich would never return, and for two other young Russians it would be a bittersweet end to one life and the beginning of another. Grigorovich was not alone, however. There were others who also would feel the outburst of wrath that soon was to come from deep within the Kremlin, and Vladimir Markoff was among them.

Vladimir Markoff was listed in the Bolshoi Troupe Directory as the Director of Transportation and Travel. The Active Soviet Agent file at the headquarters of the Central Intelligence Agency in Langley, Virginia, showed him to be much more than that. The file revealed that the troupe's Director of Transportation and Travel was really *Major* Vladimir Markoff, age 42, of the Komitet Gosudarstevennoy Bezopasnosti, the committee for state security, better known in the west as the KGB.

Major Markoff, a handsome, trim, dark-haired man, was the officer in charge of security for the ballet troupe. Under his immediate command, and traveling with the troupe, were forty-two other trusted KGB agents. The KGB not only maintained surveillance of troupe members, but also recruited and groomed the ballet groupies, usually older women, who flocked to each performance, into becoming Soviet sympathizers, as well as performing various acts of covert reconnaissance in and around the defense plants and military bases in the three cities the troupe would be visiting. Los Angeles had been particularly rich in opportunities for both kinds of work. The past three weeks had been busy but rewarding for the major. He was confident that the First Chief Directorate would be pleased with his efforts.

The major was at the small oval table in his ninth-floor room, writing what appeared to be an innocent letter to his wife and children in Moscow—only he wasn't married. Coded in the rambling text of his letter were instructions to a KGB mole that had been in place in Southern California for over ten years. Even Markoff did not know the man's identity, only his code name, Shadow. Before the afternoon was over the letter would be placed in a drop by one of Markoff's lieutenants. The Major carefully went over the letter and mentally reviewed the planned drop. He wanted to be certain he had not overlooked anything that might return to haunt him. Markoff was never able to relax fully in the United States. He knew from the moment the troupe's Aeroflot flight crossed into Western airspace over Germany nearly three months ago when the troupe departed Moscow for New York that he, along with every other Russian on the airplane, would be under the constant surveillance of the FBI and the CIA. He had no doubt that the title of Director of

Transportation and Travel afforded him little in the way of cover. Both the FBI and the CIA knew his face and his fingerprints, but unless he was caught in the act of overt espionage or linked directly to a conspiracy by another confirmed agent, his visit to the United States would likely go undisturbed. He knew that the FBI thought they could learn more from surveillance than from confrontation. He also knew that the FBI did not torture or use drugs on foreign agents, but he still dreaded the idea of spending years in an American prison. Even if his arrest resulted in nothing more than a prompt order to get out of the country, it meant he would never again be sent on a mission to the United States, and that meant severe career damage.

The Major was finishing his letter when a knock sounded at the door. Markoff instinctively tensed. He glanced at the letter and for a brief moment considered destroying it, but it had taken him nearly an hour to write.

The knock at the door sounded a second time. "Who is it?" Markoff questioned loudly. There was no hint of accent in his flawless English.

"Comrade Dneprovsky," a heavy voice answered in Russian from the other side of the door.

"Igor, you idiot," Markoff growled as he pushed the letter beneath a briefcase on the table and moved to open the door.

He had the night lock in the locked position as well as the safety chain in place. They would have bought him valuable seconds if needed. Markoff flipped the lock open and unlatched the chain. He opened the door to reveal KGB Agent Igor Dneprovsky. Dneprovsky was a tall, broad-shouldered man with wide-set dark eyes and a flat forehead.

"I'm sorry, Comrade Major," Igor said in Russian.

Major Markoff pushed by Dneprovsky to look quickly up and down the carpeted hallway. It was vacant and quiet. Grabbing Dneprovsky, the major pulled him inside and closed the door.

"Igor," Markoff warned, turning to the hulk of an agent, "if your father wasn't a general in the Soviet Army, you'd be digging potatoes."

"Major, I—" Dneprovsky stammered in Russian before Markoff cut him off.

"English!" Markoff barked loudly. "In America we speak English. That way we don't tell the world we're Russian. Do you understand that?"

"Da," Dneprovsky nodded.

"What?" Markoff demanded, glaring up at the agent, who was at least four inches taller.

"Ah, yes—yeah," Dneprovsky answered in heavily accented English.

"Now, what do you want?" Markoff questioned, walking back to the table near the window, where he picked up his cigarette pack and shook one out.

"Ah," Dneprovsky said as he struggled awkwardly with the English words, "Comrade Pronnikov reports that as of 10 A.M.—"

"Who?" Markoff interrupted sharply as he paused from lighting a cigarette. Markoff had briefed his men on the importance of never using the true names of fellow agents on foreign soil. He knew the CIA as well as the FBI had listening devices planted throughout the hotel and that the innocent-looking vans parked around the block were constantly bombarding the walls with sonic and microwaves.

Dneprovsky nodded and blinked his eyes in frustration. He stood stiff with his arms at his side, looking much like an overgrown boy in the principal's office. "I'm sorry," he said in English. "Our friend outside has counted six cars and two vans this morning."

Markoff knew Dneprovsky was talking about the FBI

surveillance vehicles, and he also knew it was likely that the FBI was deliberately giving them the easy-to-spot vehicles while others went undetected. Moscow had already confirmed that two of the bellboys and the maid that had cleaned his room were FBI agents. Markoff was amused to think the FBI had made his bed for him. It was a game, but a deadly serious one. "Did our friend get the license numbers?"

"I'm sure he did," Dneprovsky answered.

"Maybe they're here because the Jewish Defense League is planning another demonstration," Markoff offered with a puff of cigarette smoke. It was more for the FBI than it was for Dneprovsky.

"There seem to be many Jews in Los Angeles," Dneprovsky agreed.

"It's the weather," Markoff said looking through a part in the window curtain at busy Jefferson Boulevard.

"Jews like smog?" Dneprovsky countered soberly.

Major Markoff looked to the big man and smiled. Dneprovsky did not understand the humor the major found.

"It's not the smog," Markoff explained patiently. "It's the dry, treeless hills, the boulders, the arid climate, the sunshine. It's very much like parts of Israel."

"Do they have smog in Israel?" Dneprovsky questioned seriously.

Markoff studied the man for a moment. He was amazed at how sober and dim Dneprovsky seemed to be. He gave up on any further attempt at small talk. "Grigorovich has a workout scheduled for one o'clock," Markoff said. "See that the dancers have ample protection. And afterward, except for those dancing tonight, they may have three hours of free time."

"Three hours. Yes, I will see they understand."

"And make sure each group has a Soviet guide with them," Markoff cautioned. "We wouldn't want anyone getting lost in this big city, would we?"

"No, we wouldn't," Dneprovsky agreed.

"And tell Comrade Koslov I would like to speak with him before the workout," Major Markoff said to Dneprovsky. If he seemed impatient with the young agent, it was because he was preoccupied. He knew it was his task to see that the troupe's remaining two days on American soil passed without incident.

*   *   *

Nearly a block away, inside an aging blue van with fading stenciled yellow lettering that read, "Los Angeles City Street Maintenance," a balding FBI agent in gray coveralls adjusted his earphones as he fine-tuned a dial on a bank of electronic amplifiers. "Check and see if we have a Koslov on the list," he said to his younger partner, who pushed the last of a doughnut into his mouth.

"Koslov," the younger FBI agent repeated as he turned to a computer keyboard in the cramped confines of the van. The keys clattered with their loose plastic sound as the agent typed the name into the machine. As he pressed the "enter" button, both agents turned their attention to the computer's small display screen. On the screen, in soft green letters, the computer spewed out the information with an accompanying electronic chirp.

```
KOSLOV, LEONID, NMI
M/CAUC   BLK   BRN
6'1"   174   DOB 7/19/47
CTZ   SOVIET   DOD-179LS7KL
OCUP   BOLSHOI BALLET
        MAJOR SOLOIST
```

```
POLIT/STAT   SENIOR OFFICIAL—
             BOLSHOI UNIT OF THE
             YOUNG COMMUNIST LEAGUE
             PROLETARIAN
MARIT/STAT   SPOUSE; KOSLOVA, VALENTINA
ENTRY USA   7/23/79   NYC   AEROFLOT
PRIORITY 5   NEG/CON   FBI-K1971947
TIC/87 DAYS        EST/DEP   9/17/79
CUR/LOC—UNI/VER HILTON
             3540 S. FIGUEROA
             LA   CA   USA
             11:29 AM   PST      9/14/79
END.
```

The young FBI agent studied the readout on the screen. "Looks like our friend Leonid is one of the troupe's political heavy hitters."

"Kind of a party ramrod, huh?" The older agent suggested.

"You know what they say in Russian," his younger companion smiled. "'The party's never really over.'"

"I'll be glad on Monday when this party's over and this bunch of Bolshoi ballerinas are on their way back to the Motherland."
"Only two days to go, partner."

*   *   *

The message to see Vladmir Markoff was waiting at the desk when Leonid Koslov and Viktor Lazarev returned from a mid-morning jog in nearby Exposition Park. The lanky Leonid was still dressed in his sweats, but the message from Markoff said, "Urgent." Everything the KGB did was urgent, and Leonid knew that Vladmir Markoff was ranking KGB. He also knew from experience that an urgent message meant that the major simply did not want to be kept waiting.

Gentle mood music played in the elevator as Leonid rode it to the ninth floor of the University Hilton. Alone in the car, he glanced at the message in his hand. It showed Markoff was in room 914. Leonid smiled. Yesterday the major was on the eighth floor, and the day before that on the tenth. *Only the KGB would be so paranoid in America*, Leonid told himself as he reflected on his morning run. He left the hotel with Viktor Lazarev, the troupe's Assistant Artistic Director, Leonid's only trusted friend in the dance company other than his wife. Together they had headed south on Figueroa Street.

The two Russians, neither of whom spoke but the poorest of English, ran south for almost an hour. Leonid quickly noticed they were in an all-black neighborhood, not because of any ghetto-like appearance, but because all he saw were black faces. He was surprised to see them driving by in what he knew to be the most expensive of American automobiles, watering manicured lawns, and talking with smiling neighbors, or walking dogs.

As the two Russians paused for a red traffic signal at Florence Avenue in their now perspiration-stained sweats, they were joined by a powerful thirty-year-old black man in red shorts who wore a blue sweatband around his glistening forehead. "Hey, man, what's happening?" The black man flashed at them through white, even teeth.

"What's happening?" Leonid said with a puzzled look and a heavy Russian accent. The light changed to green and they jogged on. The black man now jogged with them.

"I think it is a black American expression, and not necessarily a sincere question," Viktor Lazarev said to Leonid in Russian as the trio of two Russians and the black American continued their jog.

The glistening black man gave the two Soviets a wary look when he heard Lazarev speak in Russian. As he continued to jog abreast of them he said, "Hey, you dudes aren't from the Vernon Avenue fire station, are you?"

"No," Viktor answered, "We are not fire persons."

"Well, what kind of persons are you?" The black man smiled.

"We are Bolshoi," Leonid said with his accent.

"Uh huh," the black man said, eyeing the two suspiciously as they continued to run. They were nearing another intersection. "Hey, listen, you two have a good one," the smiling black face said. "This is where I turn off. Two blocks from my lady's house, if you know what I mean—be cool."

"What's happening?" Leonid answered in reply but the black man was already out of earshot.

The two Russians turned west for three blocks and then north on Hoover Street. Leonid continued to drink in the sights and sounds of Los Angeles' black neighborhood. In Russia he had learned that black Americans lived on the edge of slavery, jobless men and women wallowing in crime and abject poverty, not really free, but chained to the heel of an exploitive capitalistic society. They had taught him that in Russia, but his eyes were telling him those were lies. The homes, the apartments, the duplexes, the laughing children, the teeming school yards, the markets, and the array of stores all combined to tell a different story, and the story was one of freedom.

The sights and sounds of freedom made Leonid's laboring heart pound even harder as the forbidden thoughts crept into his consciousness...could he be free? If this was where the black American poor lived, then they were better off than the wealthy whites in Russia. It seemed to be a happy place. He did not consider Russia a happy place. There if you laughed, you usually had to explain why. Here laughter, like life, was free. Flushing with the heat of guilt, Leonid pushed the fleeting thought from his mind and ran on.

The midmorning mass at the Vernon Avenue Sacred Heart Catholic Church had just ended, and the congregation was spilling out onto the sidewalk when the two Russians jogged by. Leonid noticed the people seemed unashamed and unafraid as they moved from the open doors of the church. Some even dared to loiter and talk. A priest was standing in the open doorway shaking hands and talking when Leonid noticed an approaching black and white police car. His stomach muscles instinctively tensed. He had seen Russians who dared loiter near a church in Moscow. They were beaten and dragged away by the police. Now it seemed the illusion that America was different was about to end, but it did not. The surprised Leonid watched as the priest on the steps of the church waved to the uniformed officers in the patrol car. The tense Leonid watched in awe as the officers smiled and waved back. Leonid ran on in silence, but his mind was a symphony of thought.

After running another six blocks Leonid glanced at Viktor and with labored breath said, "This is a beautiful place."

They ran on in silence for another block before Viktor answered. "It would seem a nice place to live," he said matter-of-factly.

It was a daring statement, and Leonid knew Viktor's heart was dreaming too. They did not speak again before reaching the hotel.

The chime on the elevator sounded as it reached the ninth floor, bringing Leonid's mind back from his run. He stepped out as the door opened.

"Come in," Major Markoff said in response to Leonid's knock at the door. The major was sitting at the table near the window reading a copy of the Los Angeles Times and drinking a cup of coffee.

Leonid opened the door and stepped inside. "Good morning, Vladimir," he said to the major, noticing the television set was on. An introductory theme to M*A*S*H was playing, as a group of military men and women rushed toward a helicopter that settled in for a dusty landing. Leonid concluded it was some type of documentary on the American military and that was why the major was watching it. In reality, the major, knowing he was being monitored by the FBI, had the television set on to mask the noises and voices in the room. It didn't really stop the FBI— it just made their job a bit more difficult, and Markoff felt obligated to do it.

"Leonid, my friend," Markoff smiled with practiced charm. "Come, sit, enjoy a cup of coffee with me."

Leonid crossed to where the major sat near the window. His instinct was to fear the man, knowing the power he wielded, but his friendship always seemed so sincere. His knowledge of classic dance was impressive, and he always spoke with great respect of Leonid's performances. Leonid wasn't sure if he was trying to be a good friend or just being a good agent. He hoped it was both.

"If you don't mind, Vladimir," Leonid said, "I'll stand. I'm swimming in sweat. I just finished my morning run."

Markoff folded his paper and laid it aside. "Yes, you and Viktor, wasn't it?"

Leonid guessed the major had seen them from his vantage point near the window as they left the hotel. "Viktor and I often run together," Leonid granted him.

"I wish I could join you," Markoff said studying the tall Leonid, "but I tore up a knee playing soccer a couple of years ago. Butcher of a surgeon made it even worse."

"I'm sorry to hear that."

"Oh, it's not that bad—at least during the summer. Winter! Well, that's another story."

"Perhaps you should have it checked here in America. I have heard they have some fine medical facilities," Leonid suggested.

Markoff smiled and chuckled at the thought. "Perhaps a Bolshoi knee would be important enough for that—I don't think mine is."

"Perhaps Grigorovich could offer you some advice," Leonid added. "Magda, Valentina's friend, had a knee problem, and he found us a doctor in Moscow."

"Maybe I'll talk with him," Markoff said, closing the subject as his mind turned to the business of the day. "You'll be going to the workout this afternoon?"

"Yes, of course," Leonid answered.

"I would like you to take a few minutes and talk to the entire troupe about our last few days here in the West. We've been here now nearly three months. Many of us have taken on all the trappings of capitalism. Sort of a 'when in Rome' cavalier attitude. This is not unusual. The allure of the West is very sweet and very strong, but it is also very deadly.

"You and your troupe are dancers, not diplomats or soldiers, and as such you are seldom prepared for the West. Here, you cannot believe what your eyes see or what your ears hear. It is time for us to pause and clear our minds and once again take the posture of true Soviet citizens."

The major drummed his finger on the tabletop as he continued. "There will be a great deal of press gathering for our departure on Monday as well as for the final performance on Sunday night. I would be very pleased if none of the troupe were again seen wearing Sasson jeans, Nikes, or Willie Nelson tee-shirts."

"I will make sure they remember they are Bolshoi," Leonid assured him, straightening his stance as he said it, "and that they are representative of the modern Soviet man and woman."

"I knew I could depend on you, Leonid," Markoff smiled, picking up his coffee cup. He sipped it and returned it to the table. "After the workout I have offered three hours of free time," he paused and offered his reassuring smile. "But you and Valentina may stay out until ten."

"Thank you, Vladimir. I appreciate your thoughtfulness," Leonid answered.

"Enjoy your workout," Markoff said dismissing him.

Leonid turned to the door. As he reached it, Markoff offered almost as an afterthought. "Oh, Leonid—"

Leonid paused and glanced back at him.

"Be careful," Markoff cautioned. "That black man you talked to today on your run. He could have been, and probably was, CIA."

Leonid managed a timid nod as his face and ears flushed with the heat of guilt. The KGB had been watching him all the time. But where were they? What else did they know? Did they know his secret thoughts? Was he suspected? He knew the major's remark was a warning. "I will be careful, Vladimir," Leonid forced from his tight throat. "Thank you."

Major Markoff nodded and picked up his newspaper to resume reading. Leonid stepped out the door and closed it behind him.

Nine miles north of the University Hilton where the Russians were housed, in the Eagle Rock section of Los Angeles, the bearded George Rollins climbed into the cab of his tattered flatbed truck and silently prayed that the battery had not gone dead again. He did not suspect the twelve volts in his battery held the fate of Major Vladimir Markoff of the KGB. George twisted the key. The engine groaned, turned over slowly, and then roared to life.

2

A Chance Meeting

THE FLATBED FORD TRUCK was eleven years old when George Rollins found it in a salvage yard in East Los Angeles — and that was three years ago. To the casual observer the truck was nothing more than junk. To George it was an answer to prayer. The body of the truck, although dented and faded, was intact, as were the drive train and transmission. The fact that it had three flats and a blown engine had simply made it easier for George to argue the price down. He was unemployed at the time, so financing the truck had been difficult, but not impossible, and after five visits to the salvage yard, Sal DeSilva, the barrel-chested owner, agreed to defer monthly payments until George got the truck running.

A sixth visit by George to DeSilva's Salvage got the truck towed to his home in Eagle Rock. There George spent nine days, working late into the night, ignoring the cold spring drizzle, under the hood of the truck, which was parked at the curb in front of his modest two-bedroom home.

George finished work on the truck engine on a cool, dreary Sunday dawn. He had worked all night but he drove his wife and daughter to church, in the truck, later that same morning. His was the only flatbed truck in the church parking lot, and it had drawn a number of less-than-pleased looks, but George didn't notice. He was too happy. Now George Rollins could become what he had always wanted to be, an independent businessman.

At age thirty-two George was best described as a free spirit. He was a handsome, sandy-haired man with long hair and a full beard. To the world it looked as if George were locked in a time warp. His red neckerchief, headband, and faded Levi's gave him a definite sixties hippie look. But to his critics George would offer a smile and answer, "Jesus had a beard. If it was good enough for Him it's good enough for me."

The past few years had been difficult for George. His independence had kept him out of the traditional labor market, and although he respected those who punched time clocks and worked nine-to-five jobs, he knew he never could. George knew that most men lived to work. Their work, what they did, what they were, became the primary motivating factor in their lives. With George it was different. He worked to live. Life was more important to him than how he earned his living, and it was out of this unorthodox ethic that George Rollin's decision to go into business for himself grew. His eleven-year-old truck was the beginning.

George had been drawing unemployment when he bought the flatbed truck with the hope of going into business for himself. He was soon to find out that the bureaucratic system that managed the so-called Employment Development Department was not designed to further independent entrepreneurial efforts. Quite the contrary, once George proudly announced to his case worker that he intended to go into business for himself, his benefits were promptly canceled. George was irate. "You mean if I sit around and can't find a job I'll continue to get paid?"

"For twenty-six weeks, with a possible twelve-week Federal extension," the clerk answered.

"So I could get paid for thirty-eight weeks?" George pressed.

"That's correct."

"But if I wanna get off unemployment and go to work for myself, you stop my benefits?"

"That's the rule, Sir."

What George lacked was operating capital. He had the idea for his independent business. He had the opportunity. He had the truck. What he didn't have was the money. But he did have determination.

That was the spring of 1976. Major Vladimir Markoff of the KGB had been organizing an intelligence network in Beirut, Lebanon. Seventy-two hundred miles to the west, in northeast Los Angeles, George Rollins was mowing lawns, trimming trees, and collecting aluminum cans. The two men were forty months from meeting, but George's determined resolve had already set the course.

After five weeks of knocking on doors, seeking lawn work and recyclable trash, George had the three hundred dollars he needed to launch "Rollin's Roadside Wholesale Produce." After filling the flatbed's thirsty gas tanks, George headed for the Los Angeles produce mart, deep in the heart of the inner city. There, in the early afternoon, after the rush of heavyweight early morning buyers from the major supermarket chains were gone, the mavericks, the small independents, would move in and buy the rejected, picked over, sometimes day-old, remains. The unwritten slogan among the major produce sellers in the mart was "sell it or smell it." They weren't in the business of storing produce, and as the day wore on and the lettuce wilted they sold. George Rollins was among those buying.

When George left the produce mart his laboring, coughing, smoking flatbed was piled high with a collection of lettuce, cauliflower, cucumbers, tomatoes, potatoes, peppers and onions as well as apples, oranges and cantaloupes for bait. He drove north on the freeway through the Cahuenga Pass and into the sprawling San Fernando Valley. There he drove up and down the streets, searching for what he hoped would be the right spot. Finally he found a vacant lot along Victory Boulevard, not far from a major intersection. He pulled the truck into the lot carefully, making sure he allowed room for customer parking, and set the parking brake. George climbed out of his truck and put up his first hand-painted sign. "Going Out of Business."

It was George's first day of roadside sales, but to him he was now one day closer to another dream that was already building in his heart and that was the dream of owning his own store, so in reality he was going out of business—the roadside business.

George had arrived for the all-important afternoon drive time and he had no sooner parked his truck than he had a passing motorist pulling over and picking over his truckload of produce. George's marketing savvy told him there was just something in Americans that made it difficult for them to drive by a fruit or produce stand. George also found that standing near the curb and eating an orange added more fuel to this natural phenomenon. He also discovered that it was very effective to give away apples and oranges to motorists when the traffic backed up from the nearby intersection. If they didn't buy something then, after he gave them free bait, he found many came back the next day.

"You reap what you sow," George smiled when someone would ask why he gave away fruit.

The success or failure of George's roadside produce was based on buying cheap at volume and selling that volume at a hundred percent mark-up. It worked, and worked well, and from his first day George enjoyed a profit. It wasn't always a large one, but it seldom failed to cover his costs and more often than not, at the end of each week, George was able to put a few dollars in savings.

George was now into his third year of roadside produce sales, and if his truck held together and inflation didn't eat another third of his profits, as it had the year before, he was hoping this would be the year he would be able to buy his own store.

It was mid-September, and that meant the usually predictable Los Angeles weather went a little crazy. A cool ocean breeze could sweep in a humid air mass, and once it collided with the static stale air standing in the Los Angeles basin, billowy cumulus clouds would climb skyward through the veil of smog. These same cumulus clouds would draft the humid air up into the higher elevations. Then much to the surprise of the tourists in convertibles below in the land where it seldom rains, they would be drenched with the noisy downpour of a thunderstorm. It was Friday and it had been a week of thunderstorms in the valley. Three out of four days so far, and the morning paper was predicting once again, late afternoon thunderstorms.

If there was something Californians hated more than rain it was mud, and George's parking spot along Victory Boulevard had been turned into a sea of mud. Sales for the week had plummeted. With rain forecast again for the day, George would buy less, he told himself as he backed the noisy flatbed from the driveway beside his house. He backed partway into the street and then stopped and honked the horn. A moment later, Sasha, George's twenty-eight-year-old wife, and Kim, his four-year-old daughter, stepped out of the house and climbed into the truck.

At twenty-eight Sasha Rollins was a raven-haired, dark-eyed, attractive woman—a first generation American, born of Russian parents, who as Christians, had fled the Soviet Union in the early thirties. She was fluent in both Russian and English, but there was seldom an occasion to use Russian in Los Angeles. Her parents, proud to be Americans, and glad to forget their bitter years in the Soviet Union, never stressed Sasha's Russian heritage, and as a young wife she was much more interested in her husband and child than she was in a Communist nation that was half a world away.

It was at a Youth for Christ rally that the two had met. To George, Sasha was an answer to prayer, and he never had any doubt that one day she would be his wife, although it took him nearly three years to convince her of that.

George had a nomadic, adventurous spirit that naturally shunned responsibility, while Sasha was stable and dependable. Out of their pairing came a union that complemented the best in each. They were truly of one mind and one spirit.

The strength and durability of their marriage would soon be tested as they were thrust into the international limelight, but as her husband drove his flatbed truck south on the Pasadena Freeway toward downtown Los Angeles, Sasha wasn't thinking about international affairs. "George," she said as the truck passed beneath the Hollywood Freeway overpass, "could you drop Kim and me at the Broadway downtown while you pick up the produce?" Sasha had four dollars in her purse. She had never bought anything at the Broadway, but it was fun to look.

"Promise you'll be out front at three?" George asked with a glance at his wife.

"We promise," Sasha assured him.

George eased the flatbed truck into the right lane and took the Sixth Street exit into downtown Los Angeles.

The empty flatbed pulled to a stop across the street from the towering Broadway complex. George dug in his pocket and pulled out a collection of change. Kim stretched out an open palm. "That's for an ice cream," George smiled, dumping the coins into the eager hand.

"Thank you, Daddy," the little girl said, clutching the change to her chest.

Sasha leaned toward her bearded husband for a kiss. "Four years old, and she's already got you wrapped around her little finger."

"Like mother, like daughter," George smiled and kissed his wife.

"See you at three," Sasha said, reaching for the door handle.

"Hon—" George called.

Sasha paused.

"Next year," George said in an apologetic tone, "you'll be able to do more than look."

Sasha offered an understanding smile in reply, "George, I don't mind. I want the store as much as you do."

"Right," George answered, "but next year you're done looking."

"I love you too," Sasha said and opened the truck door to slide out.

"Bye, Daddy," Kim added quickly as the door swung shut.

The flatbed roared, puffed blue smoke, and rattled off into the traffic. Sasha watched it fade in the distance and then looked to the sights and sounds of the inner city. The buildings towered into the sky, tall columns of concrete and glass. The sidewalks were alive with a sea of passing faces, and the street was a stream of buses, trucks and cars. It was a busy, noisy place, and Sasha drank it in. Here she was no longer a woman with four dollars and no credit cards. Now she was an attractive, dark-haired woman with her child who was shopping in downtown Los Angeles. For a brief hour or so she would have no problems and no responsibilities. Sasha knew she was weary. She could feel it. George had seen it too. It was beginning to show in her eyes. Together they had worked long and hard, and if they could only hold on for a little while longer—and Sasha knew they could—it all would be worthwhile; nevertheless, she was tired. A few hours of window shopping with a lively four-year-old would help, Sasha told herself as she glanced at the traffic signal. It winked to a green "WALK." "Come on, Honey," Sasha said, leading her daughter across the street by the hand.

The entrance to the Broadway Mall was a spacious arcade of

specialty shops. A crystal waterfall and a smooth black sculpture filled the towering space. Splashes of color covered the walls, and the tinted glass in the ceiling bathed the entryway with soft, warm light. Along with Kim, who now had her ice cream cone, Sasha window-shopped the arcade. They watched kittens in a pet shop window, selected the shoes of their choice in another window, and after Kim had finished her ice cream, browsed in a toy store. Kim's birthday was only two months away, and Sasha made mental notes of the dolls her daughter selected. Baby Newborn seemed to be the winner. Sasha had her own idea as to how Kim's desire for a newborn could be satisfied. She promised herself she would mention it to George later. After all, Kim was now almost five. It was time.

After the arcade came the Broadway store. Sasha sprayed her neck with cologne from a sampler in the cosmetics department on the first floor and then headed for the escalator and women's fashions on the third floor.

In the women's department Sasha browsed from one section to another. Kim shadowed her mother's movements, checking the texture of fabrics, considering colors, examining price tags as if she could read them. Sasha looked at bathing suits, bathrobes, women's dresses, and finally sports clothes. She was looking through a rack of designer jeans when she heard the voices — a man and a woman talking casually in Russian. Sasha had grown up in a house filled with Russian language. Her immigrant parents still spoke to one another in Russian at home, but it was a language that one seldom heard in downtown Los Angeles.

Surprised, Sasha turned and looked. The man was tall, athletic looking, in his early thirties. His hair was coal black, and so were his eyes. The woman with him, standing at his shoulder, was younger, pretty, and blonde. She was trying on a sweater. "It looks very nice," her companion said to her in Russian.

Sasha noticed another man. He wasn't far from the couple

speaking Russian, but unlike them he was dressed in a suit and tie. He was a sober, powerful looking man. When he glanced at Sasha she quickly looked away. She considered saying hello to the couple, but the man made her feel uneasy so she decided not to. Maybe the man was nothing more than a chauffeur for the couple who apparently were tourists, Sasha concluded, returning her attention to the rack of jeans in front of her. Anyway, it was none of her business and she was ready to forget them when her four-year-old tugged on her sleeve. "Mommy!"

"What, Honey?" Sasha said, glancing down at her daughter.

"Those people talk like Poppa," Kim announced proudly, pointing a finger at the Russian couple.

Sasha quickly pulled her daughter's pointing finger down. "Shhhh!" she warned. "It's not nice to point at people." Sasha looked at the couple. They had not noticed, but their sober companion had, and he was burning a look at Sasha and Kim as he stood, arms folded, glaring at them.

Sasha took her daughter by the hand and walked away.

In the casual wear department, Sasha selected a sixty-dollar dress and decided to try it on. A girl could dream, even if she couldn't buy. "Mommy is going to try this on," Sasha told her daughter as she sat her down in a chair outside the entrance to the dressing rooms. "And I want you to wait right here, OK?"

Kim climbed obediently into the chair. "Mommy, when you're done can we go see the kitties again?"

"If you're a good girl and wait right here."

"I will," Kim promised.

In a dressing room cubicle, Sasha slipped out of her clothes and into the dress. It was fresh and crisp and smelled of sizing. Sasha liked the feel of it on her shoulders. She ran her hands over it to smooth the wrinkles away. It made her feel very feminine.

Opening the door of the small cubicle, Sasha stepped into the dressing room hallway. There she had seen a full-length mirror, and before her fantasy ended she wanted to look at herself. Sasha was surprised to find the attractive blonde Russian girl standing in front of the mirror, studying a blouse she had on.

The woman was fair-complected with high cheek bones and intense green eyes. Turning to pose and look over a shoulder at herself in the mirror, the girl noticed Sasha. "Oh," she said as if caught doing something wrong.

Sasha caught her look of alarm. "I'm sorry," she said in Russian, "I didn't mean to scare you." The language came as natural as English.

The blonde girl's look of alarm quickly faded to a smile. "You speak Russian?" The girl questioned.

"Da," Sasha answered. "My parents are from Russia."

"But you are American?" The blonde pressed. The curiosity was evident on her face.

"Yes, I was born here."

"It's strange," the blonde smiled. "You speak Russian but with an American accent."

"I seldom use it anymore," Sasha explained. "Only when I'm with my parents."

"Your parents—" the blonde questioned, "they must be very wealthy to be out of the Soviet Union?"

"No," Sasha smiled. "They are not rich. My father was a farmer near Grodo. He raised pigs and potatoes. One night he took my mother, and they walked over the mountains into Poland. How did you get out?"

"Me? I have not. I am still a Soviet citizen," the blonde answered.

"You are here on vacation?" Sasha asked.

"No," the blonde smiled. "I am Valentina Koslova. I am here with the Bolshoi ballet."

"Oh, yes," Sasha said. "I saw on television that the ballet was here."

"Do you attend ballet?" Valentina asked.

"No," Sasha admitted with a smile. "My husband is not a ballet fan."

"Your husband—" Valentina questioned, "is he Russian?"

"George?" Sasha giggled. "No, George Rollins isn't Russian. He's an American."

Valentina's green eyes searched Sasha's for a moment, then she spoke. "You are an American but you have a Russian heart."

"I suppose that's true," Sasha agreed.

"May I know your name?" Valentina asked cautiously.

"Oh, I'm sorry. My name is Sasha."

"Sasha," Valentina repeated with a smile. "It is a pretty name. My grandmother was named Sasha."

"Mommy!" The small voice called from the entry of the dressing room.

Sasha turned to her daughter. "Come here, Honey."

The little girl darted to her mother to hug a leg.

"This is your daughter?" Valentina asked.

Sasha knelt beside Kim, who dared a look up at the attractive Valentina before burying her head on her mother's shoulder.

"This is Kim," Sasha said, "and she's almost five years old."

"She is blonde," Valentina smiled. "Like her father?"

"Yes," Sasha agreed. "She's Daddy's girl."

"That means she's part Russian and part American," Valentina suggested with a smile.

Outside the entrance to the dressing room an impatient Leonid Koslov paced back and forth. Being surrounded by a collection of lifelike female mannequins clad in a variety of provocative Western styles was enough in itself to make the lead Bolshoi soloist uneasy, but added to that were a number of female shoppers and the presence of the menacing, humorless KGB agent, and the result was a very nervous Leonid Koslov.

Leonid glanced at agent Sergei Romanovich, who stood only a few feet away. Usually the shadowing KGB agents assigned to them showed some thoughtfulness and discretion, but Romanovich was an exception. He simply did not care what they thought, or what anyone else thought. He stayed close. Usually so close the garlic Romanovich was fond of drove everyone else away. Leonid decided a direct approach in an effort to break through to the man. He offered a smile and moved to him. "It seems here in the West the women are very pampered."

"I have no interest in what Western women are," Romanovich answered dryly.

"I was just making a cultural observation," Leonid defended.

"No," Romanovich disagreed soberly. "You are not making an observation. What you are making is an attempt to befriend me so I might relax my surveillance of you and your wife, but I warn you, Comrade Koslov, it will not work."

Leonid turned to move away, shaking his head in disgust. Romanovich reached and grabbed him by the arm. "You may fool the others," he said with his garlic breath, "but I can see through you. I've listened to your phony political talks. They're just like you, Koslov, they have no guts. I know where your heart is, and if

I gave you a chance you'd run like a rabbit."

Leonid glared at the burly agent. He reached and pulled the man's hand from his arm. "What was that you called me? 'Comrade' Koslov, wasn't it? I know someone who would be very interested in hearing that you called me Comrade here in the middle of a major Western department store."

"No one heard," Romanovich defended through clenched teeth.

"Convince Markoff of that," Leonid suggested. "You claim you know my heart, Romanovich. Well, I likewise know yours, and I won't become a stepping stone for your next promotion—and after today that may never come." Leonid turned and walked away. Romanovich glared after him. Angry breath hissed through his flared nostrils. He secretly vowed revenge.

Leonid's stomach muscles were in a knot. He was livid. His hands trembled with anger. He took in several deep breaths and held them in an attempt to calm himself. He had lowered himself to Romanovich's level, and he already regretted it. He was an artist, not a thug. He was on the edge of becoming what he hated most, and he knew he had to regain control. He walked to a rack of blouses and pretended interest in them. A sales clerk approached him.

"May I help you, Sir?"

"No," Leonid said, forcing a smile, hoping his English would not fail him. "My wife—" he hesitated, glancing at the dressing room.

The clerk saw he was struggling for the words. "You're waiting for your wife?"

"Yes," Leonid nodded.

"Well, if I can help you with anything while you're waiting, just let me know." The clerk smiled and moved away.

The woman's courtesy touched Leonid when he needed it most. Her smile and sincere offer to serve him were so simple, yet so foreign to life in the Soviet Union. He looked around. The women's department was dotted with a variety of shoppers. There were the young, the old, the children. They shopped, smiled, chatted, laughed. They were relaxed and happy, and Leonid hungered for more of it.

Here, Leonid told himself, no one was followed by thugs with garlic breath. They weren't threatened. They didn't face prison for a careless remark, or an opinion of their own. Here they were free, and as he thought of it Leonid remembered his morning run. He had seen freedom. No matter what anyone ever said, he had seen it. He knew it was real, and he could think of little else.

In the dressing room area Sasha pushed on her shoes and stepped out of a cubicle. Kim was at her side. "Valentina," Sasha called, "I must leave," she said in Russian. "It's been nice talking to you."

The blonde Valentina cracked open the door of a dressing room cubicle across from Sasha. "I also have enjoyed our talk," she answered with a sincere smile.

The two women studied each other for a moment. Sasha wasn't sure what to say. Neither was Valentina, but there was a bond between the two, a kinship that they each felt and recognized, and it was making their parting difficult. "I hope you can come back someday," Sasha offered.

"Yes, maybe someday we will meet again," Valentina agreed, although it was edged with doubt. "That would be nice."

"May God be with you," Sasha said, and with Kim in hand she moved for the exit.

"And may God be with you," Valentina answered softly in Russian, but Sasha was gone and didn't hear.

Leaving the dressing room, Sasha saw the man again. He was standing only a few feet away from the entrance and looking even more threatening than before. She caught his look and quickly averted hers. Tightening her grip on Kim's hand, Sasha hurried by him. "Come on, Honey." She could feel his penetrating stare on her back as she moved away. Sasha hoped she would never see the man again.

But fate had a different plan.

3

The Contact

THE WEATHERMAN WAS RIGHT, much to George Rollins' chagrin. The afternoon was punctuated with a series of thundershowers that kept passing motorists in their cars. As the four o'clock hour grew near, with only eighteen dollars in sales and the rain growing heavier, George gave up.

George was drenched by the time he got all the tarps down and climbed into the cab of his truck. Kim was curled up and asleep beneath a blanket on the center of the seat. Sasha was wrapped in a sweater on the passenger's side. The inside of the truck's windows had clouded with condensation and it was cold, but to George it was a welcome relief from the chilling rain outside. Wiping the water from his face and beard, George glanced at his wife. "I give up. Nobody's gonna get soaked for a deal on a bag of potatoes on a day like this."

"He sends the rain on the just and on the unjust," Sasha smiled.

"Well, today, neither the just nor the unjust seem to want any vegetables," George answered, cranking the truck engine to life. "So we've got nearly two hundred dollars worth to find a home for."

The rain brought with it a series of freeway accidents that turned the million-dollar super highways into rush-hour parking lots. The usual thirty-minute drive from the valley to downtown turned into a monotonous two-hour drive for the Rollins in their flatbed truck stacked high with vegetables.

It was nearly seven o'clock when George pulled his truck to the curb near the Los Angeles Rescue Mission in downtown Los Angeles. The rescue mission was a haven for the homeless, hollow-eyed, gaunt alcoholics who lived like shadows along skid row. On the eve of physical and mental exhaustion, the tattered men and women would drag themselves into the mission for a night of dry sleep and a bowl of warm soup. It was not a pleasant place, but no one asked the alcoholics why. There were no qualifications, no tests, just an offer of help, with no price tag.

Climbing out of his truck, George glanced up at a large neon sign high on the Mission's wall. "Jesus is Lord," it flashed. George smiled and headed for the front door.

Inside the mission, amidst the unwashed army of tattered men, George found a gray-haired, middle-aged woman at a worn, wooden desk. A line of men stood in front of her. George by-passed the line and walked directly to the woman. The men waiting in line didn't seem to notice. "Pardon me, Ma'am, I—"

"You'll have to wait in line like everyone else," the woman said with a quick, annoyed glance at the rain-soaked George.

George caught the look and immediately understood. In the woman's eyes, he was the same as all the others in line. A drunk! "You don't understand, I'm not here to ask for help," George defended awkwardly.

"Of course you're not," the woman answered with practiced patience. "But you'll still have to wait in line—like everyone else."

George looked to the line of weary alcoholics. If they heard him, they didn't seem to care. They waited patiently, eyes downcast, shoulders slumped. And as he studied them, he realized his mistake. He didn't want to be mistaken for one of them because he felt he was better than they were. He had judged them as the woman at the table had judged him. George had to smile with the impact of the realization. "Do not judge lest you be judged. For in the way you judge, you will be judged," Jesus had said. George moved to the rear of the line to wait.

Nearly ten minutes passed before it was George's turn in front of the gray-haired woman. "Name?" the woman questioned as George stepped in front of the desk.

"George Rollins," George answered, "but I'm not here for dinner, really."

The woman put her pencil down. "And what are you here for, Mr. Rollins?"

"I've got a truckload of vegetables outside."

The woman seemed puzzled. "A delivery this late? Where are they from?"

George cut her short. "Listen, I've got my wife and little girl with me and it's late."

"You've got an invoice for us?" the woman questioned.

"I think I've got one in the truck. Could we get started unloading?"

The woman nodded. "Pull in the alley behind. I'll have the kitchen crew help you."

"Thank you," George smiled.

George backed the flatbed into the alley behind the mission. After getting Sasha a cup of coffee and Kim a cup of punch from the kitchen, George joined the Oriental cook, the black assistant cook, and two Mexican dishwashers who were unloading the array of fruits and vegetables.

In twenty minutes the truck was empty and the kitchen was full. The aging Oriental cook was picking over the vegetables like they were a treasure of gems. "Thank you, thank you, so much," the cook said to George through his yellowed, staggered teeth. "God bless you."

"God *has* blessed me," George answered. "That's why you got the vegetables." He headed for the open kitchen door and his truck, which waited in the alley.

"You have invoice?" the Oriental cook called after George in choppy English.

"No," George smiled, stepping out the door, "I don't have an invoice."

It was late, so George stopped at a burger stand just off the Pasadena Freeway and treated his wife and daughter to a cheeseburger with fries for dinner. They sat in the cab of the truck to eat, and as George asked the Lord to bless their food, he offered his thanks for the opportunity God had provided him to bless someone else. Fifteen minutes later they pulled to the curb in front of their modest two-bedroom home in Eagle Rock.

George was sitting in a chair in the living room unlacing his rain-soaked Army boots when the telephone rang. Sasha had carried the sleeping Kim in from the truck and straight to her bedroom, so pulling off his wet boot and sock, George reached over and picked up the receiver. "Hello."

"Is Sasha there?" The caller said in Russian.

George wasn't sure what the man said, but he was sure it was Russian. "Just a minute," George answered and covered the receiver with his palm. "Sasha," he called toward the bedroom.

"It's your uncle."

Sasha entered from the hallway and crossed to the telephone that George offered. "Hello," Sasha said into the receiver.

"Is this Sasha?" The male voice questioned in Russian.

"Da," Sasha answered, realizing the voice was not her uncle's.

"I am a friend of Leonid Koslov and Valentina Koslova," the caller continued in hurried Russian. "Do you know who they are?"

"Da," Sasha answered as her mind raced. "I met Valentina today at the Broadway."

George was unlacing his remaining boot. He didn't know much Russian, but he'd picked up some from Sasha and his in-laws. If he listened carefully he could sometimes follow a conversation, and seeing the sober look of concern on his wife's face, he was listening carefully.

"I tell you this in the strictest of confidence," the Russian voice said in Sasha's ear. "Leonid and Valentina would like to stay in the United States."

"Stay in the United States?" Sasha questioned. She still was uncertain what the caller wanted.

"Da," the caller answered. "Defect."

Sasha's hand went to her mouth. Now she understood, and it frightened her. George saw her reaction. "What's wrong?" he questioned.

"Can you help them?" the caller asked in Russian.

"Help them defect?" Sasha blurted in English.

George bolted to his feet. "Help who defect?"

Sasha quieted him with a gesture.

47

"Will you help them?" the caller pressed in urgent Russian.

Sasha's heart was in her throat. She bit her lip, gripped the receiver tightly. She wasn't sure she could help. She wasn't sure she could do anything. But there was a plea in the man's voice and it rang with sincerity.

"Sasha," George demanded, "what is it?"

Sasha closed her eyes, silently prayed for strength, gripped the plastic receiver with two hands and answered, "Da, I will help."

"Someone is coming," the caller breathed in her ear. "I will call back." He hung up. The dial tone sang in Sasha's ear.

"Sasha, what's wrong?" George pleaded.

Sasha lowered the telephone. George took it from her hand and hung it up. Sasha sank to the couch. She was shaken. George sat down at her side and took her hands in his. Sasha drew in a deep breath and let it out slowly. "Remember the girl I told you I met at the Broadway?" She said to George.

"The dancer?"

"Valentina," Sasha agreed with a nod. "She and her husband want to defect — stay in the United States."

"Was that her on the phone?" George questioned.

"No," Sasha answered, "he said he was a friend of theirs."

"Well, what did he want with you?"

Sasha looked to her husband, gripped his hands, "They want our help."

George was puzzled. "Our help! With a defection? What could we do?"

"I don't know, George," Sasha answered. "But the man sounded so desperate. I said we'd help."

"I heard," George said, pulling off his remaining wet sock. "I'm just not sure what we can do."

"The man said he'd call back," Sasha offered. "He said someone was coming. Do you suppose they could get in trouble? Are defections illegal?"

"I'm sure the Russians think they are," George said, massaging a cold, white foot.

"George," Sasha questioned cautiously, "did I do right? I mean was it all right to say we'd help?"

George studied his wife for a moment. It was a sober evaluation. Then he smiled and ran an affectionate finger along the line of her jaw. "Yeah," he said, "you did right. Someone asked for help and you said yes. There's nothing wrong with that."

"But what can we do?" Sasha said. Her voice was edged with apprehension.

"Well," George suggested, wiggling his toes, "seems all we can do is wait. He did say he'd call back, right?"

"Right." Sasha agreed.

George pushed off the couch and picked up his wet socks and boots. "Then we wait." He kissed Sasha on the forehead and headed for the bedroom.

While George changed from his rain-soaked clothes to a warm robe, Sasha made tea and they sat snuggled on the couch to drink it, waiting for the silent telephone to ring. The first call from the unidentified Russian had come at eight o'clock. George checked his watch, ignoring the one on the wall he had checked a hundred times before. It was nearly ten. Two hours had passed, and George was beginning to doubt the call was ever going to come. His mind was a sea of thoughts he refused to share with Sasha. Had the Russians already been caught? Were they already being rushed to the airport to be hurried out of the country? Should he call someone for help? Whom could he call? Could this be a threat to his family? Had the Russian authorities traced the call? Did they know his address? His name? What would they do?

"George," Sasha said, breaking their long silence. She had her head on his shoulder.

"Yeah?"

"I think something's wrong," Sasha added, pushing away from his shoulder to look at him.

"Why do you think that?" George countered, not wanting to admit his own fears.

"Because it's been over two hours and he hasn't called back. What if they caught them? We've got to do something."

George considered his wife's suggestion for a long moment, trying to decide what was best. Finally he looked at Sasha and took her hand. "We need to pray and ask God's guidance," George said. Sasha obediently bowed her head.

"Lord," George began, "we've got a problem. These folks have asked us for help we're not sure we can provide, but we are sure they need help. We need Your guidance in this situation, Lord. We're willing to help, but we're gonna put our trust in You and not lean on our own understanding. And as You promise in Proverbs, Lord, if we acknowledge You in all our ways, then You'll direct our paths. Amen."

"Amen," Sasha added.

"I've got the answer," George smiled.

"What is it?" Sasha demanded.

"What we need," George explained, "is legal advice."

"George," Sasha disagreed, "we can't afford a lawyer."

"No, not a lawyer," George replied. "Who do we call when we need legal advice?"

"Kirk! George, he's a detective, not an attorney."

"Yes, and as a detective he knows the law."

"But George," Sasha warned, "how's a Los Angeles police detective going to know anything about defections?"

"I don't know," George said, "but it won't hurt to ask, will it?" He reached for the telephone.

Kirk Harper, at age thirty-six, was an old-timer, a seasoned veteran of eleven years with the LAPD. He was a good cop, but a quick temper and reputation for being a bit of a rebel haunted his career. Kirk was not dissatisfied. He was happier to be known as a good cop than as a company man. "I'd sooner be right than be a sergeant," Kirk defended in a tone that didn't lack in sincerity. He was a short, powerful-looking man with dark, short-cropped hair and dark eyes. He had a quick and disarming smile that offset his serious demeanor, but when the smile faded and his jaw was set, he looked threatening. It was a "just the facts, Ma'am" Jack Webb look that Kirk cultivated effectively. He had learned command presence and used it until he could no longer turn it off. A decade of keeping the peace in the sprawling City of the Angels had turned him into an aggressive, take-charge, get-it-done, law enforcement specialist.

In the world of law enforcement, there stands a thin line between being seasoned and being cynical, and Detective Kirk Harper was at that line. He'd seen enough in his eleven years on the street to destroy anyone's illusion that justice prevails. He'd learned that crooks not only haunted the streets, but that they often wore three-piece suits, or the black robe of a judge, or even sometimes carried a badge. Kirk still believed in justice, but he was at the point where his street savvy was telling him that the system seldom delivered justice as he and other cops understood it. He was more apt to rely on his own resources to ensure justice than to rely on the courts.

Kirk was moral, fair, and he believed in God, although the term "Born Again" made him think of wimps and fund-raisers. He prided himself on being a patriot and staunchly anti-Communist. He didn't attend church regularly but respected those who did, even though he remained a little suspicious of their motives, but still he thought of himself as a Christian. The fact that he was an American and worked to preserve law and order proved it in Kirk's mind.

Cathy Harper, the former Catherine Gorsky, was the older sister of Sasha Rollins. Cathy, at thirty-three, was still very close to her younger sister, and although the two husbands, George and Kirk, were extreme opposites, the two families regularly visited one another.

Kirk often accused George of looking like a Berkeley dropout and secretly suspected it was George who had put the Carter-Mondale bumper sticker on his camper. When they were together, Kirk always insisted George drink a can of beer, and without fail, George would refuse.

"What about Jesus turning the water into wine?" Kirk argued on one of George's recent visits.

"He didn't insist that anyone drink it," George defended.

Although Kirk didn't fully understand or agree with his brother-in-law's beliefs or life-style, he respected them and knew beyond any doubt that George Rollins was sincere and trustworthy. "He may not be the best brother-in-law," he once told his partner, "but I haven't met any better."

It was Friday evening, and Kirk was relaxed in his recliner chair in front of the television set. Parked in the driveway of his comfortable Montclair Heights home was a bass boat, a pick-up truck with a camper shell, and a Datsun 240-Z. He had an attractive wife, two children, a refrigerator full of cold beer in the garage, and several thousand dollars in the bank. In Kirk Harper's mind he had it all. He wasn't sure why he wasn't really happy but he doubted anybody really was. George Rollins claimed to be, even seemed to be, but Kirk suspected that was because of some hybrid combination of hippie philosophy and Christianity that really had no foundation. He was into the comfort five cans of Coors could offer and watching a rerun of "True Grit" on cable television when the telephone rang. Kirk answered it John Wayne style. "Yo."

"Kirk, it's George. I hope I didn't wake you."

"Don't worry about it, Pilgrim," Kirk answered, continuing his John Wayne routine. "I was just sittin' here watching a little TV. Whatcha need?"

"It's a little complicated," George cautioned.

"Yeah, but so are you," Kirk countered. "So give it a go." Using his remote control he turned the volume down on the television so he could listen.

George explained how he'd dropped Sasha and Kim at the Broadway earlier in the day and that while there, Sasha had met Valentina Koslova, one of the stars of the Russian Bolshoi Ballet that was visiting Los Angeles.

"What's so complicated about that?" Kirk questioned over the line.

"Nothing," George agreed, "but consider this: We got a call about eight o'clock tonight from some Russian who asked if we'd help Valentina and her husband defect."

The line remained silent as George waited for Kirk to respond. "Kirk?" George said after an awkward moment.

"Yeah, I heard," Kirk answered. His tone was sober now. "And you're right. It's complicated."

"Can we help them, Kirk? I mean will we get in trouble?"

"What kind of help do they want?"

"We don't know," George confessed. "The guy that called asked Sasha if we would help. She said yes and then he said he had to go. Someone was coming. He said he'd call back."

"Did he?"

"Not yet."

"Where'd he call from?"

"I don't know."

"How'd they get your phone number?"

"I don't know."

"Where are these Russians staying?"

"I don't know."

Kirk brought his recliner chair to an upright position and wiped his face. "Let me make sure I got this, George. Sasha meets this Commie broad at the Broadway sometime today. Then when you get home, another Commie calls and says he's a friend of the first Commie and her husband, and they want to defect."

"Basically that's correct," George agreed.

"But you don't know what kind of help they want, where they're at, or who called?"

"Right."

"George, have you ever heard of a crank call?"

"Come on, Kirk," George defended. "When's the last time you

heard of a crank caller speaking Russian?"

"Valid point," Kirk was forced to agree. "All right, what's your plan when these Russians call back?"

"I don't have one," George admitted.

"George," Kirk admonished, "you can't deal with these Commies without a plan. They'll chew you up and spit you out. These people have ice water in their veins. You can't turn your back on them."

"Can I get in trouble offering them my help?"

"This is America," Kirk defended. "If you wanna help someone defect, nobody can stop you."

"Good," George said. "Would you help me with a plan?"

"Me?"

"You just said I needed one."

"Yeah, but me and my partner were gonna go do a little fishing tomorrow."

"Well, thanks for your advice anyway, Kirk. I appreciate it."

"Wait a minute, George," Kirk grumbled.

"Yeah," George questioned, waiting, hoping.

"I'll help," Kirk conceded reluctantly.

"Hey, Kirk, that's great," George responded.

"Uh huh," Kirk replied. "Now, if the Commie calls back before I can get over there, get some details. Find out where he is and what he wants. When do they plan to defect? Don't be afraid to ask questions."

"Got it," George assured.

"I'll be there within the hour," Kirk added with a glance at his watch.

"Hey, Kirk, I really appreciate this."

"Uh huh," Kirk answered. "See you by eleven."

* * *

Robbery Detective Steve Tilden was up to his neck in hot water. In the truest sense. Immersed in a bubbling, steaming, hot tub, Tilden sat in the backyard of his West Covina home with only his head above the water and resting on a folded towel. The cares, worries, and responsibilities of the week just past were fading as the fingers of hot water massaged his relaxing muscles.

It had been a tough week, climaxing Thursday with the arrest of the Dynamic Duo, a husband and wife robbery team who had been terrorizing small shop owners with a string of brutal daylight robberies over a five-month period.

Tilden and his partner, Detective Kirk Harper, were staked out in a mom-and-pop grocery store on West Jefferson Thursday afternoon when the Dynamic Duo, armed with sawed-off shotguns walked into their trap. Without a word, the two detectives stepped out of concealment to confront the two armed suspects.

"Police officers! Freeze!" Tilden had shouted as they lowered their thirty-eights at the young husband and wife.

The young man dropped his weapon, raised his hands, and wet his pants.

His blonde wife did not. She stood defiant, glaring at Tilden. The ominous black muzzle of the twelve-gauge shotgun she held was aimed at his midsection. Tilden stood in a combat stance with both arms extended and holding the front sight of his pistol squarely between the blonde's blue eyes. They were only ten feet apart. He knew he wouldn't miss at that range, and he also knew the shotgun fired that close would cut him in half.

"Drop the gun," Tilden warned, looking down the barrel of his thirty-eight and into the young blue eyes.

"Stuff it, pig," the drug-slurred voice answered him.

The young man beside her, arms extended skyward, was beginning to weep.

"Kill her!" Harper barked from where he stood a few feet away, covering her trembling husband.

For Tilden, time had stopped. He knew death for himself, or for the girl, was only a finger pull away. This was not his first life-and-death confrontation. His career had brought him several. On one occasion he had to kill a man. But this time it wasn't a man. This time it was a woman, and she was a young, blonde, blue-eyed woman who reminded him of his daughter Suzanne, and even knowing that it may cost him his own life, he could not bring himself to take hers. "Drop the gun," Tilden warned a second time. It was almost a plea.

The silence in the store was deafening. The air was electric, and then, the blonde pulled the trigger on the shotgun. Tilden grimaced and shuddered as the dull metallic thud of the hammer sounded. But the explosion he expected to feel as his stomach was torn apart did not come. The shotgun didn't fire.

In one quick step, Tilden closed on the girl, wrenched the shotgun from her hands, and knocked her sprawling on the floor like a broken doll.

Tilden was outside the market smoking a cigarette, trying to calm his nerves, when Harper found him. The street in front of the market was now a tangle of black and white patrol cars. The air was alive with the stereo sound of police radio.

"Hey, Wyatt Earp," Harper smiled, holding out an open palm. In it lay a red plastic shotgun cartridge with a brass base. "Take a look."

Tilden picked up the cartridge. It was live. He turned it over and looked at its base. A small pencil point indentation showed on the brass primer where the firing pin had impacted.

"Just wasn't your day, was it?" Harper said.

"I guess not," Tilden forced from a tight, dry throat.

"You shoulda shot the broad," Harper quipped and walked away.

Tilden didn't sleep Thursday night. As he lay awake in the middle of the night, the air conditioning clicked on, and for a brief terrorizing second, he was hearing the hammer of the shotgun again. The sheets were soaked with his perspiration when he finally got out of bed at 5 A.M. But now all that was fading as the hot tub did its work to relax him. Earlier in the evening he had shared dinner with his girlfriend, Terry. She had commented on how quiet he was.

It was not like Detective Steve Tilden to be quiet. He was, to those who knew him, the true tough-minded optimist. He was a good-humored extrovert who enjoyed people and enjoyed having a good time. He was a banjo player with a group of other policemen who made up a country western band called Copper Creek. Of all the things Steve Tilden was, quiet wasn't among them—he was a doer. But since the click of the shotgun hammer on Thursday, he'd turned sober and reflective. As he lay awake on Thursday night, unable to sleep after his brush with death, he tried to inventory his life as if it had ended at 2 P.M. that afternoon. He thought about his high school sweetheart, who became his wife and who gave him two twin daughters and later two sons. Now the kids were nearly grown, with plans and lives of their own, and the once-upon-a-time high school romance was now an ex-wife. Life had gone by quickly, and it had come close to ending quickly. He knew life would never be quite the same again. He had not been born again in a spiritual sense, but he realized fate had granted him a second chance. He wondered why. What remained for him to do? He hoped he would recognize it when it came, and then again he thought, relaxing in the hot, bubbling water, maybe it was just luck after all. He was on the verge of sleep when the pump in the hot tub suddenly gurgled and stopped.

"Come on," Harper called from the rear of Tilden's patio. He had the lug to the hot tub in hand. "You look like Charlie the Tuna in there."

"Get out of here before I call the police," Tilden warned.

"I *am* the police," Harper answered. "Come on, get your pants. We got us a defection to handle."

"A defection?" Tilden questioned from the hot tub.

"Yeah, a defection," Harper explained. "Like when two Commie stars of the Russian Bolshoi Ballet wanna move to the suburbs."

"You're kidding." Tilden said, reaching for a nearby bath towel.

"Would I kid my own partner?" Harper answered.

Tilden climbed from the hot tub. "It's Friday night. Do we get paid overtime for defections?"

4

The Best-Laid Schemes

"WHAT KIND OF GUY is your brother-in-law?" Tilden questioned as Harper turned the 240-Z north on the Pasadena Freeway from the inbound Pomona.

"Weird," Harper answered. He shifted the car into fifth gear and sped north toward Highland Park.

A few minutes later they pulled to the curb in front of the Rollins house. Tilden looked around, evaluating the neighborhood. It was a mix of duplexes and small frame houses. The street was lined with older cars and pickups. But at nearly 11 P.M. it was quiet. George's big flatbed was parked in the night shadow beside the house. "What's George do?" Tilden asked.

"Drives a vegetable truck," Harper said, switching off the engine.

Tilden looked at Harper in the darkness of the car. "And he's the one that's going to help two Russian ballet dancers defect?"

"Only in America, right?" Harper smiled.

There was a small, shadeless bulb glowing above the front door of the Rollins house. Harper and Tilden followed the walk toward the door. The half-hearted bark of a neighbor's dog announced their arrival, and a smiling George Rollins opened the front door before they knocked. "Have they called?" Harper demanded of him.

"Not yet," George answered, opening the door wider for them to enter.

Kirk led the way into the living room. "Hello, Sasha," he said. She was sitting on the couch. "Next time you go shopping, don't talk to strangers," he added sarcastically.

Tilden paused at the door to offer a hand to George. "Hello, George, I'm Steve Tilden. Kirk's partner."

"Nice to meet you," George smiled, shaking Tilden's hand. "Welcome to my home."

They sat in the living room and made small talk while they waited. Kirk complained that George, like always, didn't have any beer. He warned him that it was un-American. Sasha made more tea and served brownies. Tilden and George seemed to find an immediate kinship and they talked about beards—Tilden had worn one for three years in narcotics—trucks, fishing, the economy, and a wealth of other subjects as the wait drifted into its second hour since their arrival.

When Tilden mentioned that he was a member of Copper Creek, the country western band made up of cops, George remembered a guitar he had somewhere buried deep in the back of a closet.

"Steve's not interested in seeing your old guitar," Sasha said to George.

"Oh, yes, I am," Tilden defended.

It was all George needed. A few minutes later he returned to the living room with the guitar. "It might be a little out of tune,"

George said. "Do you play guitar?" he added with a look to Tilden.

"Do bears live in the woods?" Tilden smiled, taking the guitar from George to strum it. The strings plunked with dull tones as his fingers tested them. He cocked an ear and went to work adjusting and tuning each string. Finally he had it, and taking the guitar in hand, he played "Michael Row the Boat Ashore." George joined in on the vocal.

One song led to another, and soon Sasha joined in, making it a trio of voices. Harper seemed a little uncomfortable with the sing-a-long, but his foot was secretly keeping time with the music.

At the end of a song, Tilden offered the guitar to George. "Your turn."

George took the guitar and strummed it. "How about "He's Got the Whole World in His Hands?" he suggested. George led into the vocal and Steve and Sasha followed.

George followed with "He's My Rock, My Sword, My Shield," and then "Amazing Grace." They were into the second stanza of "Amazing Grace" when the telephone rang. The little trio fell silent. George quickly set the guitar aside. It was ten minutes to one. "If you guys had done one more song, I was gonna take up an offering," Kirk said.

"Sasha, you answer," George suggested as the telephone rang a second time.

The three men crowded around Sasha as she sat down beside the telephone. It rang a third time. "Get it," Kirk urged.

Sasha picked up the receiver. Her heart was pounding in her ears. "Hello," she said.

"Sasha?" The caller questioned, and Sasha recognized the

Russian voice from the earlier call.

"Da," Sasha answered in Russian, "this is Sasha."

George, Kirk and Tilden listened to the thick Russian accent as Sasha and the man talked. The call was a rush of quick exchanges, with Sasha mainly listening and punctuating his remarks with "Da," and then it was over. The line clicked silent and Sasha cautiously hung up the receiver.

"Well?" Harper demanded impatiently.

"He wouldn't tell me who he is," Sasha began. "He said he's just a friend."

"What if he's a liar?" Kirk said, thinking aloud.

"Go on, Sasha," Tilden urged.

"They have a plan," Sasha continued. "At 11 A.M. tomorrow morning, Leonid Koslov and Valentina will leave the University Hilton—"

"Where's that?" George interrupted.

"Figueroa and Exposition," Kirk answered.

"They'll walk west on Exposition Boulevard and then south on Figueroa toward the County Museum. If they're alone, you can pick them up."

"That's it?" Tilden questioned.

"Piece of cake," Kirk smiled.

"Somehow I thought there'd be more to it," George said to no one in particular.

"There may be," Sasha warned, "the man said there are many KGB agents with them, and they are dangerous."

"Do they have the right to carry guns?" Tilden said with a look to Kirk.

"Who cares?" Harper answered. "We do."

"Let's use my van," Tilden volunteered. "It has a side door. We'll use it to pick them up."

"Okay," Kirk agreed, with a glance at his wristwatch. Tilden looked at his. George pulled out his silver pocket watch and flipped it open. "It's oh-one-oh-six," Kirk said as they synchronized their watches. "We'll meet here at oh-seven-hundred."

"I'll pick you up at six," Tilden said to Kirk. "Make sure you're ready."

"I'll be ready," Kirk assured. They all said a quick good night and moved for the door. Sasha and George were with them.

"Hey," George called as the two detectives walked toward their car in the darkness, "what do we do with them after we get em?"

*   *   *

Saturday dawned bright and sunny and it was shortly after 9 A.M. when the faded white Econoline van pulled to a quiet stop behind Kline's Chevron service station across the street from the towering University Hilton Hotel. Inside the van, dressed in casual street clothes, were a nervous George Rollins, Kirk Harper, and Steve Tilden. After backing carefully to the corner of the station, just so they could see the front entrance of the hotel, they settled in with binoculars and a box of Winchell's doughnuts to wait.

Kirk had the first watch. Positioning himself near the van's curtained rear window, he lifted his binoculars, adjusted them, and studied the front of the hotel.

"Anybody know how you spot a Commie?" he questioned, watching a woman exit the hotel lobby with a dog on a leash.

"Yeah, they have a sort of a red tint to them, and they lean to the left when they walk," Tilden answered while chewing on a doughnut.

"Sasha said that Valentina is a slender blonde," George offered, "and her husband is tall with very dark hair."

"Don't worry, Kirk," Tilden laughed. "You can't miss them. They'll be the ones walking on their toes."

They ate the doughnuts, drank a thermos of black coffee, and waited.

"Do you suppose the KGB really carry guns?" George said to Kirk as the minutes ticked by. The sun was climbing in the sky and the cramped interior of the van was beginning to get warm.

Kirk shrugged, "I don't know. They're Soviet agents. Maybe, but don't worry about it. This ain't Moscow. It's Los Angeles. They're in our ball park, so we play by our rules."

A heavy thump sounded on the side of the van and then a burly black man with a pock-marked face and thick neck stepped to the open driver's window.

"Hey," he barked. "This ain't no parking lot for perverts. You wanna play kissy-huggy in the back of your van, try Hollywood."

Kirk moved from where they sat on the carpeted floor of the van, pulled his badge case from a rear pocket, and flipping it open, he stuck the gold and silver badge with its imprinted "Los Angeles Police Detective," into the man's face. "How are you this morning?" Kirk smiled.

The sober black face softened some, "I'm fine, Officer. How about yourself?"

"Fine thanks," Kirk answered. "We'll be outta here in about an hour."

"You take your time," the black man said. "I just didn't know who was back here, you understand." He waved an oily rag and moved away.

At 10:30 it was time for the bearded, nervous George to take over the binoculars and the window. He felt very much like a secret agent as he watched the unsuspecting flow of faces in and out of the hotel lobby. It was Saturday morning, so the traffic in and out of the lobby was light, but to George it was exciting and every muscle in his body was tense. He suspected every man in a sportscoat was a KGB agent. He searched with the binoculars for the telltale signs of a concealed machine gun or pistol.

"Anything cooking, George?" Tilden asked from where he sat on the floor of the van.

"All clear," George answered in a very official tone, not wanting to lower the glasses.

At 10:45 Tilden moved into position behind the steering wheel. Kirk moved to a position near the door. Their plan called for Tilden to drive while Kirk and George would throw open the side door and pull the Russian couple inside. If it went smoothly, it should only take seconds.

It was exactly 10:55 when the tense George spotted a tall, slender man and an attractive blonde woman stepping out of the lobby. "It's them," George blurted.

Both Tilden and Kirk reacted. "They're early," Kirk complained with a glance at his watch.

"They make cheap watches in Moscow," Tilden suggested.

"What are they wearing?" Kirk demanded as George continued to watch the couple.

"They're coming down the steps from the lobby to the street," George said, giving a running account of his observations. "And they're wearing matching green jogging suits and sneakers."

Tilden twisted the ignition key. The starter whined as the engine turned over but failed to start.

"They're turning west on Exposition," George said. His voice was edged with excitement.

"Come on!" Kirk growled at Tilden.

Tilden pumped the gas pedal and turned the key again. The engine turned over, coughed, and stopped.

"You've flooded it," Kirk criticized.

"Shut up," Tilden demanded, twisting the key again.

"I've lost 'em," George said as the couple, walking westbound, moved out of his line of sight behind the service garage of the gas station.

The van engine continued to turn over and sputter. "Come on," Tilden begged, twisting the key harder. Finally the engine caught and roared to life.

Tilden pulled the van to the front of the service station lot. In the rear, Kirk and George crowded to the side window to peer out. "There they are," Tilden whispered as he spotted the couple crossing the intersection of Exposition Boulevard and Figueroa Street. "Now if they'll just turn south," he added almost prayerfully.

The three men watched as the couple crossed the wide intersection. "Watch for anybody following them," Kirk cautioned.

As the couple reached the southwest corner of the intersection, they turned left and walked southbound on Figueroa. "It's them," Tilden said, breathing a sigh of relief. He pulled the van in gear.

Tilden ordered Kirk and George to lay flat on the van's floor, as he made a confirmation pass, driving by the couple as they strolled along the sidewalk. "Tall, dark-haired male, attractive blonde," Tilden said in a near whisper after he was safely by them.

"It's them," Kirk answered.

"They're playing it real cool," Tilden said as he wheeled the van left onto Thirty-ninth Street to circle back for the pickup run. "They never even glanced at us."

The white van stalked the couple as if it were a bird of prey. The couple continued to stroll, arm in arm, south on Figueroa. As soon as they were out of sight of the hotel, Tilden glanced to Kirk and George in the rearview mirror. "You ready?"

The two men were crouched by the door, ready to spring out. Kirk exchanged a look with George, who offered an affirmative nod. "We're ready," Kirk answered.

"Then here we go," Tilden said, flooring the accelerator. The van roared and raced forward toward the couple, who walked with their backs to it nearly a block away.

The van, brakes locked, slid to a smoky, tire-screeching halt beside the startled couple. Before they could react, the side door of the van flew open. The bearded George Rollins and Kirk Harper leaped out, grabbed them, and forced them inside. "Go!" Kirk screamed as he slammed the door of the van shut. It roared away. It happened in less than eight seconds.

The woman was sprawled on the van floor face down. Her husband was atop her. Twisting to the side, the tall man looked up at George and Kirk. "What is this?" he demanded.

"Shut up, Fred," his frightened wife warned. "They'll kill us."

Kirk looked to George, "They speak pretty good English, don't they?"

Tilden slowed down, wiped at his face, shook his head.

"Listen," the tall man in the jogging suit said, "I'm Fred Rogers from Fort Wayne and this is my wife, Lorraine. We're vacationing here in Los Angeles. If it's money you want—"

Tilden circled the block and returned to the spot where they had picked the couple up. After the van had pulled to the curb and stopped, Kirk opened the door. "You can go."

The couple from Fort Wayne exchanged a puzzled look. "That's it?" We can go?" The woman questioned.

"You can go," Kirk said, gesturing to the open door.

"Just get out, Lorraine," the man urged.

As the couple climbed out of the van, Kirk said, "Enjoy your visit to Los Angeles." Tilden stepped on the gas and the van roared away.

The couple stood, numbed with shock, watching the van fade in the distance. Then the man looked at his wife, "I told you L.A. was full of crazies, Lorraine."

5

Plan B

THE RETURN DRIVE to the Rollins home in Highland Park was a quiet one. The three men felt foolish and depressed. A chance to help two people find freedom had been fumbled badly. What did the Russian couple think? Did they believe the Americans were cowards who would not help? Had the KGB seen their mistake and figured out the real plan? If they had, then the Russian couple was now in serious trouble. The bravado and spirit of adventure that had carried them to the University Hilton in the morning was gone now, and in its place was a smarting, ringing, embarrassing defeat.

Sasha was waiting when the three sober men stepped through the door. "He called about an hour after you left."

"Who called?" George questioned.

"The Russian," Sasha explained. "I didn't know how to get in touch with you."

"Sasha," George said with some irritation, "you're not making sense."

"He called to say the eleven o'clock time was no good," Sasha said to the three of them.

"That's an understatement," Kirk breathed sarcastically.

"He said they would try again Sunday night," Sasha added.

"So they never were going to show this morning?" Tilden questioned.

"He said they couldn't make it," Sasha answered. "They had a workout or something."

The curtain of defeat was raised a little as the three men realized their mistake had not cost them anything other than short-term embarrassment. None, however, seemed particularly interested in telling Sasha about the incident.

Sasha had lunch ready and waiting, and she ushered the three men into the kitchen. The room was rich with the smell of hot vegetable soup. "Please sit down," she said, as she collected the bowls from the table and took them to the stove, where she ladled them full.

"Well," Tilden smiled, sniffing the steam rising from his soup. "This makes up for a less-than-fruitful morning."

"Somehow I knew it would be vegetable soup," Kirk said as Sasha set a bowl in front of him.

"Where's Kim?" George questioned, realizing his daughter was not in the house.

"Grandpa stopped by and picked her up," Sasha answered, sitting down across from her husband.

"You didn't mention the defection to your mother?" George asked.

"Are you kidding?" Sasha said, "She'd want to call out the National Guard. No, I didn't mention it."

"Good," George smiled. "Well, let me ask the Lord to bless our food."

Sasha and Tilden bowed their heads along with George. Then reluctantly, Kirk followed their lead.

"Lord," George said in a conversational fashion, "we thank You for this our daily bread, and we ask Your blessing on it, and we thank You for the opportunity You've given us to help Leonid and Valentina, and we ask Your blessing and guidance—in Jesus' name, Amen."

"Steve," Kirk said with a look to Tilden, "don't tell anyone at the station that my brother-in-law prays for Commies."

"You said the man wants us to try again Sunday night?" George said with a glance at Sasha.

Sasha nodded agreement. "He said he'd leave tickets for the Sunday night performance at the box office for Mr. and Mrs. George Rollins. If the tickets were picked up, the contact would know the plan was set and that a car would be waiting in the alley behind the Shrine Auditorium after the final curtain."

"How are they going to know what kind of car it is?" Kirk questioned.

"The man who called said he would make himself known to me by asking what time it is in Moscow," Sasha answered. "Then I tell him what kind of car it is."

It was quiet around the table as the four of them considered the plan. Then Sasha continued. "He said the final curtain Sunday night will bring a big applause because it closes the American tour."

"And where will our two would-be defectors be during all this?" Kirk pressed.

"On stage," Sasha answered. "They're the stars of Sunday night's performance."

"On stage!" Tilden said in disbelief.

73

"How will they get from the stage to the alley?" George questioned.

"The man says there's a fire door on the east side of the stage," Sasha explained. "But," she continued cautiously, "before the performance someone has to disarm the alarm on it."

The three men exchanged worried looks.

"No wonder she wanted us to have lunch before she told us," Kirk suggested. "It's our last meal."

"I don't know about this," George confessed. He was beginning to have serious doubts. Their first attempt had been an embarrassment. Now the second attempt was to be even more complex. What if they failed? Would they be creating an international incident?

"How do we get in there?" Tilden questioned. "We know there's KGB and FBI, as well as Metro and Intelligence from the LAPD. We can't just walk in. And if we did and something went wrong, we'd be fired—and my car's not paid for."

"Maybe we should call the FBI," George suggested.

Tilden and Harper exchanged a quick look.

"We call the Fan Belt Inspectors," Harper responded, "and they'll spend two days holding meetings and writing memos to Washington."

Tilden nodded agreement. "By the time they made a decision, the Russians would be gone. We've only got a little over twenty-four hours."

"Well, what do we do?" George said.

It was late Saturday afternoon when Fire Department Inspectors Harper and Tilden arrived at the Shrine Auditorium. They were both dressed in suits and ties, and each carried an official-looking clipboard. They only had one fire department badge, and that was the one Tilden borrowed from his fireman neighbor— and he wasn't a city fireman but county instead. Tilden was hoping they wouldn't look too close. He had promised his neighbor if they got caught he would swear he had stolen the badge.

Tilden was driving the detective car they had picked up at the Wilshire Division Station. Harper was on the passenger's side. "I wonder how many green Plymouths the fire department has?" Harper questioned as Tilden turned the car onto Shrine Place.

"At least one, I hope," Tilden answered, as they passed a black and white patrol car parked at the curb. The two uniformed officers in it looked at them as they passed. Kirk offered them a wave and a smile. It was not returned. "Metro?" Harper questioned.

"Probably," Tilden granted him.

There were three other black and whites along with three motorcycle officers on the block. Directly in front of the main entrance to the Shrine Auditorium, a line of well-dressed, militant-looking Jewish Defense League protestors marched in single file, carrying a variety of placards. "Free Soviet Jews"; "Keep the Bolshoi, Send Us Your Imprisoned Jews"; "Human Rights Includes Soviet Jews." Behind the protestors, flanking the bank of glass doors of the main entrance, stood a line of burly, uniformed private security guards.

Looking at all the police and the private security, Harper said, "They really pull the stops to protect these Commies, don't they?"

Tilden, to help with the bluff, drove directly to the red fire zone in front of the Shrine's main entrance and pulled to the curb. Switching off the ignition, he looked to Harper. "You ready to go to work?"

"Where's George's prayers now?" Harper said with a worried glance.

"I can hear them," Tilden smiled and opened his door.

The protestors paused to allow the two official-looking men through their file. Tilden and Harper marched through without comment. When they reached the line of security guards, one of the men reached and pulled open a glass door for them. They walked by. Tilden nodded a thank-you to the man.

Inside the lobby, Special Agent Clark Daniels of the FBI's Special Problems Unit was on duty. The thirty-four-year-old Daniels, a graduate of Duke University with a degree in accounting, was based in Washington, D.C., but his elite unit had been assigned as liaison with the Bolshoi troupe since its arrival on U.S. soil nearly three months earlier.

The tour had been hounded by the ever-present protestors from the Jewish Defense League. They were unpredictable radicals, and Daniels had nothing but contempt for them. In his mind, art and culture rose above political ideology, and the JDL, by hurling insults and threats at the Bolshoi, were embarrassing the United States government.

Folded and tucked carefully inside Daniel's suit jacket was a directive from the Department of Justice concerning President Carter's concern that any unfavorable incidents with the Soviet Bolshoi Ballet Tour may have an adverse affect upon the present high level of detente between the two countries. The concerned agencies and agents were urged to exercise the utmost vigilance and attention to duty in their efforts to maintain the security of the Soviet citizens on U.S. soil. Daniels, as a dedicated agent and American, was determined to do his part.

Special Agent Daniels spotted Tilden and Harper the moment they stepped into the lobby. They looked like local police to him. He thought the shorter, darker-haired man looked like a bully.

He would approach the taller one. He discreetly keyed his lapel mike. "Command Post, this is Delta-King-Eleven. I've got two WMAs in the lobby, probably local LEs. Stand by for further." Daniels moved for the two men.

Tilden and Harper, although they had spotted Daniels and concluded he was KGB or FBI, ignored his presence and walked toward the entrance to the main auditorium. Daniels quickened his pace to intercept them. "May I help you, gentlemen?" he called sharply to stop them.

The two men paused. Daniels moved to them. "Who are you?" Harper demanded as Daniels opened his mouth to speak.

Daniels reached inside his jacket and quickly pulled out his Bureau identification. "Daniels, FBI," he said in a polished, practiced tone.

Tilden reached inside his jacket and pulled out his County Fire Department badge. "Tilden and Harper, L.A. City Fire, Special Event Safety and Inspection." The flash of the County Fire Department badge was quick and all agent Daniels saw was "Fire Department" carved into the silver, but it was enough to convince him the two men were authentic.

"What is it you gentlemen need?" Daniels said, keying his lapel mike so the Command Post would monitor his conversation with the two men and offer feedback or instructions through his earphone if necessary.

"We're here for the quarterly Egress and Equipment Inspection," Harper answered.

In the second-story administrative offices where the FBI maintained its on-site command post, the duty officer monitoring the radio turned to his partner. "See if we've got anything from L.A. Fire on quarterly inspections."

Agent Daniels pulled a computer printout from a jacket pocket and unfolded it. His eyes scanned the pages. Tilden and Harper exchanged a worried glance. Tilden's mouth was growing cotton dry. "I don't show any authorization for inspections today."

Harper turned and gave Tilden a look of disgust, "Can you believe this?" he complained. "Same stupid thing happened when the Russian circus was here in '72."

Tilden nodded agreement and looked to Daniels. "I personally sent the teletype notification to the FBI center in Westwood two weeks ago. If you people can't coordinate proper interfacing with Special Events that's your problem, not ours."

Then it was Harper's turn. He raised his clipboard and pulled out a ballpoint. "Fire Ordinance Thirty-One-Seventy-Five gives me the authority to close this building to public access and request a hearing on an inspection denial. Now, if you want us to go out front and slap a seal on this building, you got it. How do you spell your name, Daniels?"

Daniels' confident composure was slipping. "Just a minute, fellas," he said with what he hoped was a warm smile. He turned and walked a few feet away to talk privately with his lapel microphone. "Uh, Command, can you advise on this?"

"We've looked through the fire data," Daniels' earphone answered, "and we can't find anything on the inspection."

"It wouldn't be the first time the Com-center in Westwood has deleted valuable information, would it?" Daniels suggested in a whisper. "You heard what they said about the ordinance. Firemen are not reasonable about these things."

"You've seen their identification?" the earphone questioned.

"Valid," Daniels assured, wanting off the hook.

"All right," the duty officer agreed, "let them in, but keep an eye on them."

"Seems we've found the authorization," Daniels smiled as he walked back to Tilden and Harper. Harper's forehead was glistening with sweat, but Daniels didn't notice. "So go ahead and proceed with the—"

"Egress and Equipment Inspection," Tilden answered.

"Right," Daniels agreed.

They started their mock inspection in the spacious main auditorium under the watchful eye of another FBI agent that Daniels had assigned to shadow them. They spent twenty minutes pretending interest in fire hoses, emergency door lighting, sprinkler pipes and extinguishers, making what they hoped were convincing notes as they worked. Finally the agent lost interest in them and disappeared.

Turning their attention to the fire exits, the two men casually inspected all of them before approaching the stage. They followed a dim back hallway that led to stairs backstage.

The polished, wide stage was fronted by towering, ornate curtains and covered with a soft, dim light that filtered down from several spot lamps high overhead. Walking onto the stage, listening to the sound of his own footfalls, Tilden was awestruck. He looked around, drinking in the sights and smells. Harper walked over to join him. "Looks like the top of an aircraft carrier doesn't it?"

"Can you imagine the talent, the names, that have stood where we are?" Tilden said with a look to Harper.

"No," Harper said flatly, "I can't."

"There's Barbra Streisand, Bob Dylan, John Denver, Diana Ross, Rod Stewart, Linda Ronstadt—"

"I get the picture, mister show-biz," Harper said with a smile.

"Man, if these walls could talk," Tilden suggested, "what a

story they would tell. Who knows who may have stood where we're standing?"

Perhaps important to the walls of the Shrine Auditorium was not only who had stood there, but who had knelt there. Thirteen years before the two police detectives walked onto the stage, an evangelist, lesser-known perhaps than the show-business personalities who had dominated that stage, had begun a series of meetings with prayer. That prayer, mostly forgotten by even those who heard it in person, had asked that as long as God permitted it to stand, this stage would be dedicated to Him as the scene of life-changing miracles. God was going to answer that prayer.

"Come on," Harper said to Tilden as he glanced around to make sure they were alone.

Tilden didn't move. "Can't you feel it?" he said to Harper.

"Feel what?"

"I don't know," Tilden confessed with a shrug. He couldn't find the words. "Just a feeling."

"It's probably the ghost of Christmas past," Harper said sarcastically, coming much closer to the truth than he knew. "Come on, let's finish and get out of here."

They found the fire door they wanted on the east wall of the stage. An official-looking sign on the door warned, "Caution: Emergency Exit Only. Alarm Activated When Opened." Harper played the role of lookout while Tilden knelt in front of the door and searched for the thin wires that led from the door handle to the wall. Finally he found them taped to the rear of the long, smooth bar handle. He looked to Harper to get an all-clear nod, then went to work with a pocket knife.

Tilden cut away the protective tape and pulled the two thin wires away from the pipe handle. He offered a quick, silent prayer that the alarm wouldn't go off, grimaced, and ripped the knife through the two frail wires. The wires fell apart, and the alarm remained silent. Tilden breathed a sigh of relief and quickly fingered the tape and severed wires back into position behind the handle.

Standing, Tilden glanced to Harper again. Harper nodded all was clear. Tilden depressed the handle and put a shoulder to the door. It screeched open. A shaft of sunlight sliced through the opening along with a rush of fresh air. Tilden pulled it shut. Then stepping back from it, he searched for signs of tampering. There were none. He turned and moved past Harper. "It's done. Let's go."

6

Discovered

IT WAS EARLY SATURDAY EVENING and the lights were beginning to wink on across the face of Los Angeles. In his ninth-floor hotel room Major Vladimir Markoff, shoes off and feet propped up, watched the local television news. A black reporter announced that striking bus mechanics had voted to end their twenty-three-day walkout against the Southern California Rapid Transit District, clearing the way to resume bus service in Los Angeles. Markoff shook his head in disbelief. How the United States of America, one of the two great superpowers in the world, could allow one of its major population centers to be paralyzed by a band of striking bus mechanics for twenty-three days was inconceivable to him. He simply could not understand a freedom that permitted such things. Was freedom something that allowed men who wanted a higher wage to strike and make old men, women, and children walk for three weeks? Was that freedom? Freedom was such a beautiful concept, Markoff had to agree, but it was obviously doomed to being consumed by American greed.

A knock sounded on the door. Markoff reached and turned the volume down on the television set. "Who is it?" he questioned in his flawless English.

"Room service," a muffled male voice answered from the other side of the door.

Markoff pushed out of his chair and crossed to the door in his stocking feet. He was tense. He hadn't ordered anything from room service. He stepped quietly to the peephole in the door and stared out. The fish-eye viewer revealed a young man in a red jacket. He had a tray in hand. Markoff unlocked the door. The boy stepped in. "Where would you like this, Sir?" He carried a bottle of vodka and a glass on a tray.

"Just put it on the table," Markoff answered. He signed the room service ticket while the boy put the tray on the table.

"Thank you, Sir," the young man said, accepting the ticket and pen from Markoff. "Have a nice evening," he added as he stepped out and closed the door.

Markoff didn't answer. His thoughts were on the bottle of vodka. It was a signal from Shadow, the KGB mole in Los Angeles, and it meant they were to meet. Markoff wasn't thinking about who Shadow may be. He was too much the dedicated professional for that. His mind was on why. Only the most compelling of reasons could call for such a meeting. Shadow knew that Markoff was surrounded by a horde of FBI agents intent on watching his every move, and to meet him meant that Shadow was putting the greatest trust in him. If something went wrong, the ten years of work invested in building Shadow's deep cover would be lost. Markoff was already thinking of ways he might get out of the hotel undetected.

The hotel register showed room 1006 rented to Pamela Stewart, a thirty-two-year-old corporate attorney and USC alumni from Des Moines, Iowa, in town for a three-day seminar on Constitutional Law at USC's Sheffield Center. The information was nearly all correct. Pamela Stewart was, in fact, in room 1006, and she was a thirty-two-year-old attorney and USC alumni from Des Moines, but that's where the truth ended. There was a seminar on Constitutional Law at USC—the KGB had already checked that—but Pamela Stewart wasn't attending.

Pamela Stewart was, in fact, a member of the FBI's covert surveillance unit, and occupying the room directly across the hall from KGB Major Vladimir Markoff, she was, as they say in the business, "on the point."

The three suitcases the bellman carried into the room when the attractive Pamela checked in all contained video equipment, which was now set up and in operation. A small but powerful wide-angle television lens was held in place over the peephole in the door of Pamela's room with a black suction cup. A pencil-sized coax cable led from the lens over the peephole to a nearby table, where Pamela sat monitoring a small television set and running a video recorder. She had an excellent view of the door to Markoff's room and the surrounding hallway. A listening device slid beneath the edge of her door added amplified sound to the visuals. Pamela made a note on a clipboard and picked up a small recorder. "Bellboy exited the primary's room at eighteen-seventeen hours. Apparently delivered a bottle of clear liquid. Probably vodka. Returned to service elevator east wing. Subject Markoff observed wearing tee-shirt, slacks without shoes."

The hallway was quiet as Pamela moved into her third hour of watching the door and hallway on the small television screen. She glanced at her watch. In 47 minutes Sherry Bell, posing as a girl friend, would arrive for the second three-hour watch of the evening. She was looking forward to Sherry's arrival. The bellboy had been the highlight of the past two hours, and Pamela suspected that now that Markoff had his evening's supply of vodka, he'd be drinking himself into an alcoholic stupor. She didn't really consider the Russian much of a challenge.

She was turned away from the screen, rummaging in her purse

for her cigarettes, when the door across the hall opened and Major Vladimir Markoff stepped out. A motion detector blinked a small, red warning light on a panel beside the television screen, but Pamela had turned the audible alarm to the off position. Cigarettes in hand, she turned back to the monitor just as Markoff moved for the elevator. Spotting him, Pamela dropped her cigarettes and grabbed up a nearby telephone. She stabbed at the buttons. Her eyes were glued to the television set as the figure moved casually away. "Come on, come on!" Pamela growled into the receiver.

"Hello," a male voice answered in Pamela's ear.

"Dave, it's Pam," she blurted, trying to control her excitement. "Uncle John's changed his mind. It looks like he's going to come over."

"Thanks, Pam."

The duty officer in the surveillance van hung up the telephone and keyed his radio. "Tactical units, this is Arm Chair, stand by to roll, Primary Six is on the move."

When the elevator reached the parking level, the door parted and Markoff stepped off. He was greeted by two young, smartly dressed KGB officers. They walked a few feet from the elevator before speaking. "The garage was swept this afternoon. It's been covered since then," one of the young men with a dark mustache explained. He spoke in soft Russian.

"We walked the perimeter just a few minutes ago," the other added. "We have about six guests this evening. They were alerted shortly after you left your room."

"Tell Nikolai I may be late," Markoff said to the two young men. "Have either of you seen him?"

"I understand he's attending this evening's performance," the mustache answered.

"If I've not returned by morning, or telephoned, have him call San Francisco at noon."

The two young men nodded agreement.

"Goodnight, gentlemen," Markoff said and walked toward a waiting rented sedan.

If Vladimir Markoff had to pick the thing he hated most about Los Angeles, it would have been the freeways, and now he found himself driving on one of them. The driving course he'd taken at the center outside Moscow years ago hadn't prepared him for Saturday night traffic on the northbound Harbor Freeway. The Major's palms were damp on the hard plastic of the steering wheel as he followed the sea of red taillights into downtown Los Angeles. Behind him, in front of him, and overhead were two vans, six cars, and two helicopters. The Major, were he not a rigid bundle of nerves, would have been flattered.

A street meeting in Paris, or London, or Mexico City, or in nearly any other major city in the world, did not require driving oneself, but Los Angeles was the exception. For all practical purposes, Los Angeles had no public transportation. The fact that the company running the city bus system called itself Rapid Transit was an accepted Angeleno joke. The lack of public transportation was going to make it harder for Markoff to shake the surveillance he was certain was with him, but for now he had a more serious problem, and that was finding the right exit for the transition road from the northbound Harbor Freeway to the northbound Hollywood Freeway. Studying the maze of freeway signs and arrows, Markoff was beginning to understand why so many Americans prayed.

Fifty minutes after leaving his hotel and getting lost twice on the freeway, Markoff eased his rental car onto the Sunset Boulevard exit of the Hollywood Freeway. The FBI units tailing him thought the Major was being extremely cautious, when in reality, he was simply confused.

Markoff wheeled his sedan into the parking lot of a Denny's Restaurant on Sunset Boulevard.

"Adam-Six and Eight," the Command surveillance unit called. "He's going into Denny's. Go with him."

Markoff sat down at the counter in the restaurant. He was glad to see it was busy, although the young man beside him with blue hair and earrings was a little unsettling.

"Coffee?" A busty, middle-aged waitress questioned, setting a glass of water and a menu in front of him.

"Yes, please," Markoff answered.

He waited until he was certain the FBI had men in the restaurant before he ordered a patty melt with fries. The sandwich was tasty, and he enjoyed several bites of it before he got up and walked to the men's room.

In the busy restroom he entered one of the two stalls, bolted the door, and went to work. He unfolded a golfing cap from a jacket pocket and put it on. From another pocket came a pair of dark, horn-rimmed glasses and a gray mustache.

Slipping out of his jacket, he pulled a tennis shoe from each armpit. Pushing off his polished black shoes, he pulled on the dirty white tennis shoes. He unknotted his tie and pulled it away, then turned his collar under.

Reversing his sports jacket to reveal a faded plaid pattern, he slipped it on. And, although Markoff hated cigars, he took a half-smoked one from a pocket and lit it.

Stepping out of the stall, he dropped his dress shoes into a trash can. The transition took less than a minute, and the change was remarkable. The men moving in and out of the restroom seemingly paid no attention to him.

Markoff checked his image in the mirror. He looked typical of the middle-aged drifters on Sunset. He mussed his hair a bit around the edge of his cap and moved for the door.

He puffed several times on his cigar and limped a bit as he headed for the door to the parking lot. Pushing through the door, he glanced back. No one was moving to follow.

He left the FBI watching the rental car in the parking lot and the door to the restroom as he walked undetected west on Sunset Boulevard to the theater. There, satisfied he hadn't been followed, he bought a ticket and went inside. The billing on the marquee read "Midnight Express."

The Major waited until his eyes adjusted to the darkness before he moved down the left aisle. He counted the rows carefully. Nine rows down and then four seats to the right. He found a couple sitting in the third and fourth seats. He sat down beside the woman and began to cough, sucking in air each time to make a deep, raspy lung sound. After three coughs, he cleared his throat and spat in an empty popcorn box. The couple got up and moved away. The Major moved over two seats to the right and settled in to wait.

Markoff was beginning to enjoy the picture, although he couldn't understand why the young American was finding survival in a Turkish prison so difficult. Obviously he'd never heard of Siberia. The young man was being subjected to an interrogation, and the Major couldn't help but be critical of the techniques being used. His attention was on the screen, so when a hand touched his shoulder from behind, it brought a strong reaction. "Don't turn around," the voice behind him warned. It was a woman's voice, and that surprised Markoff, but still he forced himself to relax in his seat. He kept his face forward but tried to glimpse the woman with glances to the left and right. She was sitting directly behind him, and he could see nothing of her, just the left hand on his shoulder, which was now removed. He had to smile at his vulnerability. He had come expecting to meet a man. The woman was obviously there when he sat down, but because of what he expected, he had paid her no attention. It was a lesson Markoff promised himself he would not forget. "I thought perhaps you'd dropped your wallet?" the female voice said behind him.

"No, I have my wallet," Markoff answered, and the identity of the two strangers was established.

"This morning, a call was made from a public telephone at the Shrine Auditorium," the woman said, leaning near Markoff's ear. She sounded mature, educated. He could smell her perfume but not identify it.

"Not highly unusual," Markoff suggested.

"The caller spoke in Russian—and so did the woman who received the call."

Now the woman had Markoff's attention. He straightened in his seat. Members of the Bolshoi as well as his agents were forbidden to use public telephones. All telephone calls had to have prior approval, and most were monitored. Someone had violated the order. It was important to know who and why. "Who were they?" he questioned.

"My contact at the telephone company speaks very little Russian," the woman explained, "but the caller was a man, and the call was made to a woman in northeast Los Angeles by the name of Sasha."

"What did they talk about?" Markoff demanded.

"They spoke of plans for a defection."

"When?" Markoff pressed soberly.

"As I said," the woman answered, "my contact only speaks limited Russian, but there's only tonight and tomorrow night."

Markoff nodded agreement. His mind was racing ahead. "How can we find this—Sasha?" he questioned.

"I'm guessing she's a Russian Jew," the woman offered.

"Don't guess," Markoff warned.

"My contact is searching all the telephone numbers in north-east Los Angeles for all Russian and Jewish names, particularly any with the first name of Sasha."

"We must know quickly," Markoff urged.

"I'm doing the best I can," the woman defended, "which is obviously more than the agents with the troupe at the Shrine did this morning."

Markoff knew Shadow was right. The call never should have been made. Someone had failed to cover a public telephone during the troupe's morning workout. Undoubtedly she would include it in her next report to Moscow. "I'll find the individual responsible for the lapse in security," Markoff vowed, hoping his comment would also be included in her report, but he knew the chance of that was slim, because as the senior agent, he was ultimately the responsible individual.

"I think it more important that you find the individual planning to defect," the Shadow suggested.

"Then get me Sasha's full name and address," Markoff shot back at her.

"I'll get it," Shadow promised. "Don't turn around for five minutes," she cautioned.

Markoff heard the seat behind him squeak and fold up. The air grew richer with the smell of her perfume. He heard the rustle of her dress as she moved away. He gave in to the urge and turned to look. She was already into the aisle and moving away, just a shadowy silhouette fading into the darkness. Markoff returned his attention to the screen. Now he could identify more with the young American drug dealer in the picture. They were both in serious trouble—both caught in the middle.

7

Checkmate

GEORGE ROLLINS WAS IN BED and asleep by 11 P.M. His wife, Sasha, was not. She was in the kitchen ironing her high school prom dress. It was the only formal Sasha owned, and thus the only one she would have to wear to the Sunday night performance of the Bolshoi Ballet. It was a floor-length, low-cut, green satin dress with a full petticoat, and Sasha hadn't worn it in more than ten years. She had slipped it on before getting out the iron, just to make sure it still fit. It did, much to her delight, although the petticoats gave it a definite sixties look, so she decided to wear it without them.

After Sasha finished ironing the dress, she hung it carefully on a hanger and began her search for the dress's matching purse and shoes. She found both. The only item missing was a wrap. The Sunday night performance started at eight o'clock, so it was not a matter of choice. She needed something to wear over her bare shoulders, but there simply was nothing. She owned a faded Levi jacket, a plaid three-quarter-length coat her mother gave her, and a gray weather coat George bought her at a garage sale. Well, if there wasn't anything, that's just the way it was, so Sasha accepted it and turned her attention to more pressing matters, such as her nails and hair.

Sasha Rollins was not the only one up late getting ready for Sunday night's final performance. Nine miles to the south of the Rollins residence, where George lay sleeping and Sasha sat polishing her nails, Major Vladimir Markoff was holding a tense staff meeting with eight of his senior agents.

Markoff, in shirtsleeves, was pacing back and forth in front of the sober collection of agents gathered in his hotel room.

"We face a deadline in the truest sense of the word, my friends," Markoff warned. "Either we find this traitor in our midst, or he destroys us. Either we return to Moscow to report our success, or we return in the shame of disgrace and failure. This man, whoever he is, would destroy the pride of the Soviet people, as well as our careers, without a thought. We must find him and we must stop him. I want you to put the pressure on. Work with your informants in the troupe. I want you to restrict possible suspects to their hotel rooms and put them under guard if you have to. I want security brought up to full alert, and I want no more mistakes. We have but a little over twenty-four hours remaining on American soil. All we have to do is prevent this defection."

Markoff stopped pacing and studied the faces. "It's these cursed intellectual artists," he said, almost growing angry as he spoke. "Whether they're writers, poets, or Bolshoi, they think of themselves as creative beings above any national interest. None of them have the heart, or the guts, to be true Soviet patriots. It seems they would sooner wallow in the filth and decadence of this whore-infested city than represent the pride of the Motherland, and I, were it not for our national interest, would be among the first to say give them what they want. We have no room in our midst for traitors. Do what you have to do, but find him."

*　　*　　*

94

Sunday morning dawned bright and sunny in Los Angeles, and by nine o'clock the temperature was already in the mid-seventies. In Monterey Heights Kirk Harper, unshaven, dressed in robe and slippers, was settled in his recliner chair watching "The NFL Today" and awaiting the start of the Rams-Redskins game at 10:00. In West Covina Steve Tilden was sprawled across his waterbed, asleep, with the telephone off the hook and the curtains pulled shut. In South Los Angeles at the University Hilton, the Bolshoi Ballet troupe were under orders to have breakfast in their rooms. Word had been passed shortly after 7 A.M. that only the members scheduled to dance in Sunday night's final performance were permitted to leave their rooms, and then only to board a supervised bus for the ride to the Shrine Auditorium. The others were ordered to pack for the return flight to Moscow in the morning. There were many complaints. A final day of shopping and sightseeing for those not performing was lost, but no questions or exceptions were permitted. The hallways were suddenly full of patrolling KGB agents who had been warned that there was serious trouble. No one seemed interested in asking why.

Harmon Marshal, the senior resident agent in charge of the Los Angeles office of the FBI, was sitting in the kitchen of his Pasadena home scanning the Sunday Times when the electronic pager sitting on the table sounded its call. Harmon, a big, balding man with intense green eyes and a thick neck that gave him a powerful look, reached and turned off the pager. Lenore, his wife of twenty-eight years, who sat across the table from him, picked up the telephone from the counter and offered it to him. "Would you like your coffee warmed up?" she questioned. After twenty-seven years with the Bureau, she no longer speculated on calls.

"Yes, please," Harmon smiled at his wife as he dialed the duty desk at the center in Westwood.

"Six-five-two," a male voice answered in Harmon's ear.

"This is command page nine," Harmon said to the voice.

"Good morning, sir," the voice answered, "I have a call for you from the duty officer at the Shrine Command Post. Let me patch you through."

Harmon listened to several electronic beeps, and then another voice answered. "Morning, Harmon, this is George Wills at the Shrine."

"George!" Harmon said with surprise in his voice. George Wills was his second in command, and if he was at the command post on a Sunday morning, it meant the duty officer had called a tactical alert. Harmon straightened in his chair. "What are you doing there?"

"Monitor, is this line secure?" George Wills asked before he answered Harmon.

"It's on the scrambler," a voice answered on the line.

"Thank you," Wills said, and then added, "The duty officer called a tactical alert at nine-fourteen, Harmon."

"What's the problem?" Harmon was eager for an answer.

"The duty officer got a call shortly after nine this morning from a male who identified himself as Major Vladimir Markoff of the KGB."

"He called there! How did he get the number? It's supposed to be a secure line."

"We don't know," Wills conceded, "but he called."

"Was it really Markoff?" Harmon pressed.

"Voice-print confirms the I.D.," Wills answered.

"What did he want?"

"He said he wanted to meet with an official of the United

States Government—as soon as possible."

"Good Lord," Harmon blurted. "Could he be the one planning to defect?"

"We think that's a possibility."

"Call the center, George," Harmon ordered. "Have the bird pick me up in twenty minutes. And find a secure location for a meeting with Markoff."

"We're already working on it."

*   *   *

George Rollins, sitting in the Sunday morning service, tried to concentrate on the pastor's sermon, but his mind kept racing ahead to the events waiting for him later in the day. He glanced to Sasha at his side, then slid his hand into hers. She gripped it affectionately. Her hand was warm and soft. He was considering telling Kirk and Steve Tilden that he'd decided that Sasha couldn't go. It was just too dangerous for her. What if something went wrong? Sasha would be on her own. Alone. Could he, should he, as a responsible husband, allow Sasha to be part of the defection? There was no doubt the KGB was dangerous, even on American soil. He almost wished Sasha had never met the girl. What right did she have to ask them for help? If the situation were reversed, would the Russian couple help them? He didn't think so. Maybe they should have called the FBI. They could be violating international laws they weren't even aware of. He could think of a number of good reasons for them to give up on this would-be defection and few, if any, for them to continue. He'd already given up a full work day on Saturday, and after a week of rain, that was going to prove costly.

And what about after the defection? How long would these people want to stay with them? Could they afford it? Would he have to miss more work? He just didn't have time. Plus, they could be on their way to creating an international incident just because it made them feel macho. George's mind was made up. As soon as they got home from church, he was going to call Kirk and tell him the whole thing was off. He wasn't going to get involved with the Soviets. He had no right. The most he would consider would be allowing Sasha to call the FBI. If they wanted to pick up on it, that was their business. They got paid for it. He didn't. His mind made up, George turned his attention to the pastor's sermon. He realized for the first time that the message this morning was from Luke 10, the familiar parable of the Good Samaritan. He was quoting Jesus' words from verse 37: "Go and do the same."

"What a challenge this is!" the pastor said. "This man freely gave of his time and his money, sacrificing *all* for someone he had never met, someone of another nationality, someone whom he had no logical reason to help. Our Lord calls us to be willing to do the same, and He is the ultimate example of this kind of sacrifice.

"What we must ask ourselves when we're asked to sacrifice for others," the pastor said as he continued, "is what would Jesus do? Did He turn people away? Did He ask, 'What's in this for me?' Was He looking for the benefit to Himself when someone asked for help?"

The pastor looked directly at George. At least George thought he did. "Will you help me?" The pastor stretched out a symbolic hand. "Will you help me? What would Jesus do?"

The pastor paused dramatically for a moment, studying the congregation. "Tell me," he challenged, "when did Jesus send someone away? Tell me, when did Jesus say, "It's none of my business'? Tell me, when did Jesus say, 'I don't have time'?"

George released Sasha's hand. He was listening to every word now.

"When's the last time you found yourself in trouble and you cried, 'Oh God, help me!' and God said, 'Not now, I'm busy. It's none of my business. Take it to someone else. I don't have time'?

"He had time to carry a cross to the top of a hill called Calvary. He had time to die for you, and He has time when you cry, 'Lord, save me!' So when someone comes to you and says, 'Will you help me?' ask yourself, what would Jesus do?"

The pastor went on, but George didn't hear anymore. He had bowed his head.

*   *   *

It was almost eleven o'clock when the call came into the FBI command post at the Shrine Auditorium. The FBI was ready, and less than thirty seconds into the call, they confirmed it was coming from room 1007 at the University Hilton. There was no doubt that the caller was Major Vladimir Markoff of the KGB.

Harmon Marshal had arrived an hour earlier. He took the call. "This is Harmon Marshal. I'm the Resident Agent-in-Charge of the Los Angeles office of the FBI."

"I would like to meet in ten minutes," Markoff said over the line. "I'll be in Exposition Park. I'll be wearing a brown sweater, and I will be alone."

George Wills was standing at Harmon Marshal's side, listening to the conversation on an earphone. He tapped Harmon on the shoulder and shook his head no. Harmon glanced at Wills and then spoke into the receiver. "I would prefer to meet on Washington Boulevard. There's a motel near the intersection of—"

"I can't do that," Markoff interrupted. "I'll be in the park in ten minutes." He hung up.

The FBI had to work fast, but when Major Markoff stepped out of the University Hilton eight minutes later, there were twelve agents and eight cars surrounding Exposition Park, which was two blocks away.

The park, a green belt punctuated with the marble Grecian-looking buildings of the Los Angeles County Museum, was dotted with shade trees and a rolling expanse of grass. Markoff strolled into the park from Figueroa Street. He was wearing an open collar and a brown cardigan sweater he'd bought in Chicago. He walked west into the heart of the park, smoking a cigarette under the watchful eyes of the FBI.

Markoff heard the car approaching from behind, but he didn't bother to turn and look. In a moment it rolled slowly by and pulled to the curb a few yards ahead of him. Behind the wheel was a balding fifty-year-old with a thick neck. He opened the car door and climbed out. Markoff recognized the man from the picture in the intelligence briefing book. "I'm Harmon Marshal," the man said as Markoff reached him. "What can I do for you?"

"Walk with me," Markoff suggested, wanting to get away from the car.

Four sets of binoculars, a thirty-five millimeter camera, and a television lens followed the two men as they cut across the green lawn in a patch of shade.

"My government," Markoff explained as they walked shoulder to shoulder, "is very concerned about the development of a situation that could have an adverse affect on our relationship with the United States."

"We have the expression here in America that's called 'the bottom line,'" Harmon Marshal answered. "It means let's talk about what we came here to talk about."

Markoff stopped and turned to face Harmon. "All right," he said in perfect English. "The bottom line is, we have solid evidence that the FBI has lured a member of the Bolshoi into defecting."

"That's a lie," Harmon defended. "The FBI is not involved."

Markoff smiled. His bluff had worked. Now he knew the FBI had knowledge of the planned defection. "But you do know of it?"

"We have information, as you have information," Harmon surrendered cautiously.

"Don't you think," Markoff went on, "since the FBI has knowledge of the planned defection that it's going to look like you were involved?"

"Not at all," Harmon said, rejecting the idea.

"And don't you think it goes against your own presidential directive regarding the FBI role in preventing such incidents which could harm detente."

"You seem very well versed on our policy," Harmon Marshal answered.

"Mr. Marshal," Markoff smiled, "I'm on your turf. I have to know how you play the game."

"We don't consider freedom a game," Harmon defended.

"Please," Markoff said, "let's not get into a political debate. We are two professionals with a job to do. Now, let me make my position clear. I'm interested in leaving Los Angeles tomorrow morning with the same number of Soviet citizens I arrived with. You can help me do that by insulating our dancers from any contact with American citizens."

"Let me make my position clear, Major," Harmon answered. "We're not in the business of helping the KGB with anything."

"I think you need to consider the personal and professional

impact of your choice, Mr. Marshal," Markoff warned. "The Soviet Ambassador to the United States in Washington is at the Department of State right now, and he's telling the Secretary of State about our meeting. And within the hour the Secretary of State will telephone the President— Now, if the defection takes place and I disclose that you knew, who do you think the President's going to thank for the new state of relations between the world's two superpowers? You will not get the promotion you've been hoping for before retirement, and a President, who will likely be re-elected to a second term, is going to be very unhappy with you."

The two men studied each other for a long moment. It was a sober, chilling evaluation. Then Harmon Marshal broke the silence. "You sound like a desperate man, Major."

Markoff answered with a shrug, "Perhaps today I am, Mr. Marshal, but tomorrow it may be you." The Major turned and moved away.

"Major," Harmon called.

Markoff paused and looked back.

"We thought you were the one."

The Major considered the suggestion soberly. Then a smile crept across his face. "And have to drive these freeways? Never." He turned and walked on.

8

Showtime

SASHA STARTED GETTING READY a little after four o'clock. After church she and George had stopped by her parents' house for lunch. It was a Sunday tradition. At Grandma's insistence, Kim had been left behind for a promised trip to the zoo. Sasha had asked her mother if she would keep Kim overnight, explaining that she and George were going out in the evening. "Is it something special?" Her mother asked. "We think so," Sasha answered.

George had his orders to stay out of the bedroom as Sasha began to fill the tub with hot water. He tried finding something on television to take his mind off the two-hour wait that remained before Kirk and Tilden arrived, but after searching the channels and finding nothing of interest, he switched it off. He got out of his chair, deciding he'd change the oil in the truck. Reaching the front door, he changed his mind. It was a messy job, and Sasha would be irritated that he'd done it on Sunday. George paced the living room. Glancing at the wall clock, he forced himself to admit he was nervous.

George was comfortable with the idea that he was doing what the Lord would have him do, but the peace he had come to expect after finding God's will was eluding him, and it was adding to his uneasiness and worry. As he paced, smelling the scent of warm soap from his wife's bath, he spotted Sasha's Bible on a table at the end of the couch. He picked it up. Wisdom was what he needed, so he opened the Bible to the book of Proverbs. If he could just grasp some insight into what was going to happen tonight, George told himself, then he'd have a peace about it. It was the unknown that was worrying him.

The words on the page spoke to his spirit as loud as a voice. In Proverbs 22:17-19, he read,

Incline your ear and hear the words of the wise,
And apply your mind to my knowledge;
For it will be pleasant if you keep them within you,
That they may be ready on your lips.
So that your trust may be in the Lord,
I have taught you today, even you.

"So that your trust may be in the Lord"! George had always marveled at the way God's Word so accurately dissected the thoughts and intents of his heart. It was hard to explain to those who did not share his love for Scripture, but George felt that what he appreciated most about the Bible was its ability to deliver the kind of stinging rebuke that cut to the very soul. The peace that flooded him when he yielded in his heart to those rebukes could not be described with human language.

It was a quest for that kind of peace, he suddenly realized, that had led him to open the Bible just now. *"So that your trust may be in the Lord"*! He had taken his eyes off the Lord, and had let himself get caught up in the circumstances of this drama. His worries this morning and the lack of peace in his heart just now were symptoms of that. He was forgetting the most important part of his relationship with God: that the just shall live by faith.

Lord, George prayed in his heart, *forgive me for not trusting. You have clearly led us this far, and You've confirmed to me that it's Your will that we help these people. Help me to trust You for the outcome.*

As he prayed and the peace of God flooded his heart, George was suddenly both confident and keenly aware that God had been in control of the details of this defection from the beginning, and he knew that ultimately nothing could defeat His purposes.

* * *

"If anybody calls, tell 'em I'm at a defection," Kirk Harper called to his wife as he stepped out the door.

When Kirk arrived at his brother-in-law's house in Highland Park a little before six, Steve Tilden's white van was already parked in front. He found George and Steve sitting in the living room. There was a little small talk, and tension was running high. "Here's what we've come up with," Tilden said to Kirk as he sat down with them. "Sasha is going to pick up the tickets. George will drive the van and make the pickup in the alley."

"Why George?" Kirk questioned.

"Because the cops just might recognize you or me," Steve answered.

"Oh!"

"I'll cover the east end of the alley in my VW," Steve added, "Kirk, you take the west end with your Z."

"How do we communicate?" the bearded George questioned.

"Just raise your hand when you have a question," Kirk suggested sarcastically.

"I mean once we're there," George defended.

"Once we're in position, that's it," Steve warned. "We'll keep an eye on you, George, but until you move, it's your ballgame."

"Thanks."

"As soon as you've got the two Commies in the van and pull away," Kirk assured, "Steve and I will close in to run interference—just in case the KGB or somebody should wanna play chase."

George acknowledged with a sober nod.

"George is going to drive me back to my house to pick up the VW so we'll have to leave a little early," Steve said to Kirk.

Kirk nodded agreement, "Let's meet at Winchell's Donuts at Adams and Figueroa."

"And after the pickup do we drive straight back here?" George questioned. His voice was edged with apprehension.

"Unless your two passengers haven't had dinner," Kirk teased. "They may wanna drive through McDonalds and get some chicken McCommies."

Steve patted George on the knee. "We'll meet back here and decide what's next."

George nodded agreement as he tried to sort out the remaining questions that were playing tag inside his head.

"I guess that about covers it," Kirk suggested.

"Wait a minute," George said. "What about Sasha?"

"We covered that," Kirk answered. "She's picking up the tickets and going inside."

"But how does she get there?" George countered.

"Couldn't you drop her off out front?" Kirk suggested.

"But how would she get home?" George questioned.

"What other vehicles do we have?" Steve asked.

"Just my truck," George answered.

"Can Sasha drive the truck?"

*   *   *

The green, low-cut satin dress contrasted sharply with Sasha's fair complexion and dark hair. Looking at herself in the bedroom mirror, she had to admit she enjoyed getting dressed up. She hoped George would think she was pretty. She could hear the men talking in the living room, and she was a bit anxious about going out there, but she'd stalled as long as she could. She glanced in the mirror for a final check, raising her chin just a bit for effect. She was pleased with what she saw. Except for her bare shoulders. It wasn't that her shoulders were unattractive, it was the fact she still needed a wrap. Then she remembered her Grandmother's lace tablecloth.

Sasha turned and moved to the bottom drawer of the bedroom dresser. The lace tablecloth was a special gift from Sasha's mother on her wedding day. It had been handmade by Grandma Magdalene who was too old and too frail to leave Russia when the others fled. She had thrust the treasured lace into her daughter's hands the rainy night they packed to leave. "Take this," the old woman insisted. "Give it someday to your daughter."

The tablecloth was folded carefully and tucked beneath Kim's baby clothes in the bottom drawer. Sasha uncovered it and lifted it from the drawer. The once alabaster lace was now an antique beige, but the delicate handwoven pattern denied age. Returning to the mirror, Sasha faced it and let the lace unfold and slide down over her shoulders. The traces of lace, green satin, and soft skin blended beautifully, and Sasha smiled with pleasure at the sight of it. The tablecloth, fashioned so long ago by the bony fingers of an elderly Russian woman in the mountains of the Ukraine, transformed itself into a high-fashion lace shawl on the shoulders of a young American on her way to an evening ballet performance. Grandma Magdalene would have approved.

"Sasha," George said in a near whisper as she stepped from the bedroom with the lace around her shoulders. He stood up, staring at her. Steve and Kirk followed George's lead and stood. "You—you look beautiful," George stammered as the satin rustled and Sasha crossed to him. The scent of her perfume was rich in the air.

"Thank you," Sasha purred and took George's hand.

George was awestricken with his wife's beauty. He tried not to stare.

"We have some good news and some bad news," Kirk said to Sasha.

"Let's start with the good news," Sasha smiled at him.

"The good news is you look like you should be wearing glass slippers," Kirk answered.

"And the bad news?" Sasha questioned, holding onto George's arm.

"The bad news is you have to drive the vegetable truck."

"We're sorry," Steve added sincerely. "There just isn't any other way."

"I don't mind," Sasha answered, squeezing her husband's hand affectionately, "I ride in it every day."

"Just make sure you're home by the time the clock strikes twelve," Steve added with a complimentary smile.

George backed the big flatbed truck from beside the house into the street and set the brake as Sasha waited at the curb. Climbing down from the cab, George brushed the smooth vinyl seat clean with a hand and let the door stand open.

"Good luck," Steve called to Sasha as she moved for the truck. He stood at the curb waiting with Kirk.

"Break a leg," Kirk added.

Steve gave Harper an annoyed look. "You say 'break a leg' to someone going on stage."

Kirk shrugged, "Well, I didn't know what to say for a defection."

"Nosdrovya," Sasha answered.

George helped Sasha up into the cab of the truck, behind the wheel. Sasha carefully tucked the green dress in around her. "You look beautiful," George said to her as he stood on the running board at the driver's open door.

"I love you too," Sasha smiled.

"Be careful, Sasha," George cautioned.

"I will," she assured.

George leaned toward her and they kissed. When their lips parted, he stepped down and closed the door of the truck.

Sasha glanced down at her husband from behind the wheel of the truck. "George, wipe your lipstick off." She shifted the big truck into gear and pulled away. George wiped at his lips and offered a final wave.

"Best looking truck driver in L.A." Steve said as the truck turned the corner at the end of the block and disappeared.

"Let's go to work," Kirk suggested soberly, as George reached them.

* * *

Sasha's drive on the freeway was uneventful. Only in Los Angeles could a woman in a green satin formal drive a vegetable truck on a freeway and go unnoticed. She drove south on the Pasadena Freeway to the southbound Harbor. It was early evening, and the traffic was light as the sun drew near the horizon in the west. As Sasha neared the Exposition Boulevard exit, she eased the truck into the right lane.

Major Vladimir Markoff was sitting near the south windows in the coffee shop of the University Hilton enjoying an after-dinner cup of coffee before his departure for the Shrine Auditorium. He paid no particular attention when the flatbed truck drove by on Exposition Boulevard. Markoff glanced at his watch. In a little over three hours, the curtains would close on the last American performance and less than twelve hours after that they'd be on a flight to Moscow. It seemed the security alert was paying off. Everyone except the cast for the final performance was confined to his room, and the cast now at the Shrine was under heavy guard. The would-be defection had been stalled. There was still the problem of identifying the traitor in their midst, but that would be much easier handled in Moscow. He was certain the director would want the names fast. Perhaps he could start the screening interviews on the flight to Moscow. He signaled a nearby waiter for a check.

The parking lot adjacent to the Shrine Auditorium was a polished, glistening sea of Mercedes, Cadillacs, and Lincolns. Those drawn to the Bolshoi's final performance were the aristo-crats of Los Angeles. Twenty-two-year-old Manny Mendoza, the red-jacketed parking lot attendant stationed at the pay gate entrance to the lot, hoped to earn at least a hundred dollars in tips from the "fox and tux crowd," as he called them. Thus, he was a little surprised when the faded flatbed truck slowed and turned toward the entrance to the lot.

Sasha had driven around the block three times in search of a parking space. The spots she found were either too small for the truck or posted "No Parking — Tow Away Zone." The parking lot was her only hope. She prayed the attendant wouldn't turn her away as she pulled to a stop beside him. The young Latin seemed less than thrilled to see her. "You wanna park here?" he said in disbelief, eyeing the truck.

"Yes, please," Sasha answered. Already two cars had pulled in behind her and were waiting.

"I don't have room for no trucks," Manny responded, glancing at a third car that pulled in behind the flatbed.

"Please," Sasha pleaded. "There's nowhere else to park."

A horn sounded behind the truck. Manny knew the fox and tux crowd didn't like waiting.

"OK, OK," Manny blurted. "But I gotta charge you double, because you take two spaces."

"That's fine," Sasha answered.

"Ten fifty," Manny demanded.

Sasha picked up her purse from the seat of the truck and opened it. Ten dollars and fifty cents was a new shirt for George, or shoes for Kim. She dreaded spending it on parking, but there was simply no choice. Sasha opened her wallet as a horn honked for a second time behind the truck. Her heart was thumping in her chest, which made her fingers tremble as she counted the bills. She found a five and three ones — eight dollars. She pulled it out, snapped open her coin purse. She found a quarter, a dime, and two pennies. She drew in a breath and looked to the young attendant. "I'm sorry, I only have eight-thirty-seven."

An impatient horn sounded again. Manny was angry. With a line of cars building behind the truck, it was obvious he couldn't have the woman back up, and he didn't have time to go unchain the exit. "Give me the money."

Sasha dumped the eight dollars and thirty-seven cents into Manny's hand.

"Park in the back," Manny barked.

Sasha was glad to leave the truck behind and melt into the crowd that moved toward the front of the Shrine Auditorium. Now, except for the fact that she was alone, she didn't feel so different.

The lines in front of the auditorium were huge, and the sidewalk was a sea of smiling, laughing faces. Everyone seemed to know everyone else. There was a great deal of superficial kissing and hugging as fur- and gold-draped women greeted one another and men shook hands. Sasha felt very alone and very frightened. Her anxiety doubled when she saw there were three ticket booths. The lines were long at each booth, and she wasn't sure what to do. She chose the closest line and moved to the end of it to wait.

The line moved forward at a snail's pace, and twenty minutes passed before Sasha stepped in front of the agent in the booth.

"May I help you?" The gray-haired woman in the booth intoned mechanically.

"I have some tickets waiting," Sasha smiled. "The name is Rollins."

"Will-call is at booth B," the woman answered.

"Booth B?" The disappointed Sasha questioned, "Which one—?"

"Center," the woman added impatiently.

"Thank you," Sasha said and moved away.

The second line added another fifteen minutes to Sasha's wait, and as she stood in line, a woman behind her commented, "My, what a lovely shawl. Did you get that here in Los Angeles, Honey?"

"No," Sasha answered. "It's from Europe."

"I do most of my shopping there, too," the woman smiled.

Finally it was Sasha's turn at the window. The clerk was a young man in a white shirt and bow tie. "I have tickets waiting, the name is Rollins. Sasha Rollins."

The young man searched through an indexed box labeled "Will Call." Sasha watched through the glass, holding her breath, as the fingers leafed through the names. Finally he stopped, pushed the box aside and looked to Sasha. "Sorry, I have nothing under that name. Perhaps you should check with reservations."

Sasha was heartsick and desperate. "They've got to be there," she protested.

"Either buy a ticket or step aside," the young, sober face behind the glass ordered.

Tears of frustration and defeat began to well in Sasha's eyes. *Oh, God, help me*, she cried silently.

"Young lady," the woman behind Sasha said, tapping her on the shoulder, "the very same thing happened to me once. Have him check under your husband's name. It's a chauvinist world, you know."

"Check under George Rollins, please." Sasha pleaded. Her voice was thick with emotion.

The young man in the bow tie was visibly irritated with the suggestion, but he gave in to it and reached for the box. Sasha continued to pray as the fingers searched. Finally they stopped and the young man's eyes went to Sasha's. "Was that George Rollins?"

"Yes," Sasha answered apprehensively.

"Mr. and Mrs. George Rollins," the young man smiled, pulling two tickets from the file. "Enjoy the program, Mrs. Rollins," he said, sliding the tickets beneath the glass.

Program in hand, Sasha found her seat just before the house lights dimmed and the music came up as the curtains parted. The program's cover displayed a picture of Leonid Koslov and Valentina Koslova, the stars of the evening's performance of Swan Lake. Sasha ran a finger affectionately over the edges of the picture and looked to the stage.

Sasha had never seen live ballet before, and she was awed by its beauty and grace. Leonid, as Prince Siegfried, with his long arms and legs, seemed to move through his dance with a fluid grace that ignored the law of gravity. His movement and mood were linked to the music as if it were his own breath. His command of the stage held the five thousand in attendance in reverent silence as if they were prisoners, and, for the moment, they were.

Leonid Koslov knew this was his last performance with the Bolshoi Ballet, and he had secretly vowed to his wife, Valentina, it would be his best. To Leonid it was more than Swan Lake. To him it was a heartfelt swan song. He was giving all that his years of Bolshoi training and discipline enabled him to give, and it was magnificent.

Valentina Koslova was a beautiful Russian woman, and to those who had seen her dance before, her beauty was no surprise —but this night was different, this night she was glowing. Only three people in the crowded auditorium knew why. Valentina, her husband Leonid, and Sasha Rollins, who sat in the midst of the audience, waiting.

Sasha had been so drawn into the performance that she was shocked when intermission came. The thunder of applause and the shouts of appreciation that accompanied the curtain's closing brought her back to the chilling reality of the evening. For the audience, the intermission was a social break, a time to see and to be seen. Thus most moved for the aisles and the lobby. Sasha Rollins was not among them. Fearing she might miss the contact if she left her seat, she stayed in it. Sasha's heart was thumping so hard in her ears that it made her feel as if she couldn't breathe. The realization of what was happening shocked her. She was hyperventilating. She envisioned herself being carried out of the auditorium on a stretcher, blue-faced and unconscious. She held her breath in an effort to calm down and combat it. The psalm that she'd read the night before at bedtime came to her. *"Wait on the Lord: be of good courage and He shall strengthen thine heart; wait, I say, on the Lord."* Sasha silently thanked God as she calmed down.

Sitting, waiting, Sasha ran the plan through her mind. The contact would ask, "What time is it in Moscow?" And she would tell him what type of vehicle would be waiting behind the Shrine. It was so simple, she couldn't understand why she was so frightened, but realizing it and controlling it were two different things. She hoped George was all right. She prayed for the hundredth time that God would keep him safe. When Sasha raised her head to look around, she caught the man's look. He was sitting four rows ahead of her and to the right. Twisting in his seat he had his arm cocked on the seat back. He was a handsome man in his mid-thirties, and he was wearing a gray tuxedo with a red carnation on the lapel. He smiled when he caught Sasha's bashful look. She quickly averted her eyes, but then realizing he may be the contact she returned her eyes to his and smiled. It worked. He pushed out of his seat and moved for the end of the aisle. A moment later he was standing beside Sasha. He smelled of cigarettes and alcohol. "That's a beautiful dress," the white, evenly-capped teeth said with practiced charm.

"Thank you," Sasha said modestly, with a quick glance up at him.

"I've enjoyed the program," he answered, "but I'm enjoying the intermission even more."

"It should be almost over," Sasha suggested.

"Do you think so?" the man said with a glance at his gold wristwatch. "Let's see, what time is it?"

"It's a white van," Sasha said to him in a hushed, tense whisper.

The man studied Sasha for a moment. He had a puzzled look on his face. Sasha saw it. "It's a white van," she said again, thinking he hadn't heard.

A pleased smile covered the man's face, "You make up your mind real fast don't you, Honey?"

"What?" Sasha questioned.

"You want me to meet you at your van, right?" the man quizzed.

"No," Sasha said indignantly, "I'm sorry. You're not who I thought you were."

The man looked Sasha over and nodded his agreement. "I'm sorry too." He turned and moved away.

Sasha sat, eyes downcast, smarting with shame and embarrassment. She was such a fool. She had made such a stupid mistake. A mistake that could have jeopardized Leonid and Valentina's safety—perhaps even their lives. She was nearly ill with fright and tension when someone tapped her lightly on the shoulder. Sasha bolted straight with fear.

"Do not turn around," the voice warned in English that was thick with a Russian accent.

Instantly Sasha recognized the voice as the one from the telephone. She obeyed and kept her eyes on the distant stage and

116

the heavy curtains that awaited their parting for the final act.

Only seconds passed, but to the frightened Sasha it seemed an eternity before the man spoke again. "Do you know what time it is in Moscow?" he asked quietly.

"It's a white van," Sasha breathed.

It was quiet for a moment, then the man laid a hand on Sasha's shoulder. "Thank you," he said in soft Russian, and then the hand disappeared. Sasha did not turn around. A tear of emotional relief spilled and traced down her cheek.

The lights in the auditorium winked, indicating the intermission would soon be ending. The gala crowd, filled with the latest gossip and a final lungful of nicotine, began returning to their seats. Sasha, recovered some, was feeling a bit smug. She was the only one in the vast audience who knew how special this final act was really going to be—at least she was the only one until burly KGB Agent Sergei Romanovich came up the center aisle against the flow of the crowd, looking, searching, with the same menacing aura of fear about him that drenched his frame the day Sasha had seen him in the Broadway department store.

Sasha had finally begun to relax. The contact had been made successfully and she felt there was little chance of anything else going wrong now. She was looking forward to the conclusion of Swan Lake when she spotted Romanovich. His narrow, dark eyes seemed to look straight into her heart to find the plot hidden there. Suddenly she felt like a frightened rabbit trapped by a snarling, frothing hound. Her breath left her in a rush as a chill of fear shuddered up her spine. She quickly averted her eyes, praying the man hadn't recognized her. She forced a breath into her starved lungs; it was a near sob, that drew a curious look from the man beside her. She had to know if the man saw her. She looked back to where he stood and found his penetrating stare still locked on her.

The auditorium lights faded as the music came up and the curtain parted. Sasha dared a glance as the shadow of Romanovich's hulk moved up the aisle and disappeared into the darkness. She was frozen with fear. The doubt was gone. The man had remembered her.

Romanovich went to the men's room in the lobby, where he lit up a cigarette. He was desperately trying to remember where he'd seen the woman in the green satin dress. He was frustrated with a memory that just couldn't grasp the connection when the muffled applause sounded for the beginning of the final act. Leonid Koslov would be coming on stage, Sergei thought, and then he remembered! The girl had come out of the department store dressing room where Koslov's wife, Valentina, was trying on clothes—she must be Sasha, and the Koslovs were the defectors! He'd have his revenge on Koslov after all.

Sergei smiled and took a final drag on his cigarette, then flicked it on the floor and stepped on it as he set out to find Major Markoff.

9

Freedom Dance

THE THREE MEN SAT in the white Econoline van in the parking lot of the Winchell's Donut shop at Adams and Figueroa. Tilden's green VW, as well as Kirk's 240-Z, were parked close by. Each man had a styrofoam cup of coffee. George's thoughts were with Sasha. He knew that by now the contact had been made. He hoped she was enjoying the ballet. She had looked so beautiful. "Hey, George," Kirk said, interrupting George's thought.

George looked to Kirk from where he sat behind the wheel of the van. Kirk was on the passenger's side with his feet propped up on the padded dash. Tilden was sitting on the floor behind Kirk in the van's open side door. "Yeah," George answered.

"Why are you doing this?" Kirk questioned.

"Doing what?" George wasn't sure what his brother-in-law meant.

"This defection thing," Kirk answered. "What's in it for you?"

"I hadn't really thought about it," George admitted candidly.

"Is it because you're a Born-Again?" Kirk pressed.

Kirk so seldom mentioned George's Christianity that George

was surprised by it. "I'm sure that's part of it," George answered. "How about you? What's in it for you?"

"It's his bounty-hunter instinct," Tilden said from behind Harper.

"Part of that's true," Kirk added to his partner's remark. "It's a rush, a thrill, and I think that's part of why Steve and I are cops, but that doesn't fit you," he said with a look at George's long hair and headband. "You're not a cop. You look more like something left over from the Age of Aquarius."

"To be honest with you," George offered, "I wavered for a while before I decided to go ahead with this. I could think of all kinds of reasons *not* to get involved, but not many good ones for doing it."

"That's understandable," Kirk said. They were silent for a moment. "So what made you go ahead with it? You're not the gung-ho type."

"You're right, I wouldn't do it just to satisfy a craving to seem macho," George admitted. "But I just know that because of all that Christ has done for me, dying for my sins and all, I can't just turn away for selfish motives and refuse to do all I can to help someone in need."

Steve was suddenly interested. "So you're paying God back for saving your soul," he said, as if he understood completely.

"No, it's not that at all," George said. "Salvation is free, no strings attached. We can't be good enough to earn our way to heaven, and God doesn't want us even to *try* — the penalty for sin is so costly we couldn't pay it anyway. That's why Jesus paid it for us. He doesn't want us to pay Him back."

"That sounds a little too good to be true," Steve said.

"But it *is* true," George said excitedly. "In fact, to *try* to pay

Him back is an insult to Him, an act of unbelief against His Word."

"Where does the Bible say that?" Steve asked, not as a challenge, but with a tone of sincerity.

"Ephesians 2:8 and 9," George recited. "'For by grace you have been saved through faith; and that not of yourselves, it is the gift of God; *not as a result of works*, that no one should boast.' And Titus 3:5: 'He saved us, *not on the basis of deeds* which we have done in righteousness, but according to his mercy—'"

"But I always thought you had to be good to go to heaven," Steve interrupted.

"God's standard of good is perfect, and only Jesus was ever *that* good," George said. "God doesn't ask men to be good in order to be saved; He saves them and makes them good by transforming them to be more like Jesus. Eternal life is a gift, paid for by the blood of Christ." He paused a poignant moment, then continued softly when neither man said anything, "You receive that gift by faith—just acknowledge to God that you're a sinner in need of salvation and trust Christ as Savior."

"You sound like you want us to do that right here," Kirk said.

"There's no reason you can't," George replied seriously.

The next few minutes passed in silence. George prayed silently that the Lord would bless the seed that he had sown.

Kirk dropped his feet from the dash and glanced at his watch. "Hey, look what time it is," he said. "Let's get this show on the road."

"George, you go first," Steve said as he stepped out the open side door of the van. "And be careful," he added, closing the door.

Kirk opened the passenger's door and slid out. "Well, see you after the defection," he said with a wink at George. "And remember, don't talk to strangers." He slapped the metal door shut and started to move away but paused to glance back. "Be careful," he added soberly.

"I will," George promised. Kirk moved away. George drew in a breath. "Here we go, Lord," he whispered and turned the key. The starter whined and the engine turned over but failed to start.

"Pump it!" Steve shouted from the darkness.

George pumped the accelerator several times and twisted the ignition key again. The starter whined, the engine turned, coughed, sputtered, and finally roared to life. He thanked God and put the van in gear.

The face of the Shrine Auditorium was ablaze with lights, and the sidewalk in front was busy with a line of JDL protestors, the curious, security guards, and a mix of press intent on picking up color for the usually slow Sunday night news. The curb was parked bumper to bumper with waiting limousines and bored drivers. George slowed to look as he drove by, but a uniformed officer in black, polished boots and a white helmet blew a whistle and waved him on. The sight of all of it had a sobering, chilling effect on George that settled deep in the pit of his stomach. Any idea he had that this was some lighthearted adventure quickly vanished with the reality that the time was at hand.

It was a warm, moonless night, and the alley behind the Shrine Auditorium was black with heavy shadow. George wheeled the van into the alley from the west end. The light from the head-lamps swept over the collection of trash that littered his path. George drove slowly, snaking around the array of broken bottles. He had almost reached the rear of the towering Shrine when a glass beer bottle shattered under the pressure of a rear tire. George grimaced as if he could feel the jagged glass cutting into his feet. He prayed that the tire hadn't been punctured and drove on.

A single shielded bulb glowed above the loading dock at the rear of the Shrine, casting a faint light into the darkness. Beneath the light a sign warned, "Authorized Personnel Only—No Trespassing." A series of heavy padlocks hung on the big sliding door. To George's relief, there was no one in sight.

George drove slowly by the rear of the building until he could see north along the east wall. There he pulled to the south side of the alley and stopped. He switched off the headlamps and twisted in the driver's seat to study the ominous-looking dark hulk of the auditorium. A red bulb glowed in the darkness near the rear of the building on the east wall. George knew it was the fire door. He reached for the key to shut the engine off, but a sudden, paralyzing fear that the van might not start again stopped him. He decided to let it idle and pulled his trembling hand away from the key. Returning his attention to the open driver's window and the stillness beyond, he listened. From inside the auditorium came the faint, muffled music of the orchestra. "Oh, Lord, help us," he breathed in the darkness.

KGB Agent Sergei Romanovich finally found Major Markoff in the west wing of the stage, talking quietly with a costumed and dark-eyed brunette ballerina. "Excuse me, Comrade," Romanovich said, tapping the major on the shoulder. Markoff turned and gave Romanovich an annoyed look. "It's important," Romanovich assured.

Markoff leaned close to the ear of the dancer. His remark was covered by the sounds of the orchestra but the girl's eyes swept to Romanovich, then she smiled, nodded to the Major, and moved away. When she was gone Markoff turned to his agent. "What is it, Sergei?"

"I think I have found our defector," Romanovich smiled.

Markoff sobered and straightened his stance. "Who is it?" He demanded.

Romanovich turned his head and shoulders toward the lighted stage behind him where Leonid Koslov was at the apex of a high leap. "Him," Romanovich growled.

"Koslov," Markoff said in disbelief. "How do you know this?" He wanted proof.

Romanovich was ready for the questions. "Friday I escorted Koslov and his wife to a department store. His wife tried on many clothes, spending a great deal of time with a woman in a dressing room. That same woman is sitting in row twelve, seat D. There is an empty seat beside her."

"Sasha!" Markoff hissed.

"Yes, Sasha," Romanovich agreed.

Markoff's mind was already racing ahead. "Get Rozhkor, Vanagel, Barsukov, and Lisovsky to join you here on the stage." In the troupe the men were known as "The Gang of Five." They were big, humorless, powerful men that together equaled a platoon of soldiers. Markoff wanted the physical and mental edge of intimidation they could provide. "The moment Leonid and his wife have made their last curtain call I want you to take them into custody. Then along with me, you will escort them back to the hotel."

"It will be my pleasure," Romanovich smiled.

"In the meantime," Markoff added, "I'll say hello to our friend Sasha."

George pulled out his pocket watch and held it close to his face in the dim light. It seemed he had been waiting for an hour, but only ten minutes had dragged by. Heat from the idling engine and tension had George swimming in sweat. Even the bottoms of his feet were hot, and then he noticed the windshield was beginning to cloud with vapor. He leaned close to the heat gauge on the dash and strained to see it in the darkness. His heart jumped. The thin needle was against the hot peg. The engine was dangerously overheated. Steam vapor was beginning to boil out from around the hood and drift away. The engine was now laboring and running rough. George raced the engine in an effort to cool it as well as smooth its idle. His heart was pounding in his chest.

Major Markoff paid an usher five dollars to check and make sure the seat beside D in row twelve was still empty. He waited at the rear of the auditorium until the young man returned. "It's still available, sir. Shall I escort you down?"

"No, thank you," Markoff smiled. "I'll find it."

Sasha was so tense she could hardly breathe. The excitement and escape the ballet had brought her before the intermission was gone, and now all she could think of was the burly man's icy stare. But Leonid and Valentina were still on the stage, still dancing. Even if he had recognized her, they still had no way of knowing the plans for the defection. She had herself nearly convinced when a man stepped into the row, moved past the first two people, and sat down in the vacant seat beside her. Sasha kept her eyes locked on the stage and the dancers of Swan Lake, but her mind was on her purse and the knowledge that in it was the ticket for the seat beside her. Breath rushed in and out of her flared nostrils as she ran the myriad of questions and fears through her worried mind. How did he know the seat was vacant? He had come directly to it. Was he KGB? Maybe FBI? Could he be the contact? Had he been forced into coming back to change the plan? Maybe he was nothing more than a devout ballet fan who had arrived late—but maybe he'd been following her all night. The man confirmed his identity by leaning toward her. In a soft whisper he asked, "Sasha, is everything ready?"

Was it the same voice? Why did he come back? Had he seen the same man she had? Was he giving her a chance to change her mind? If he hadn't whispered she would have known, but he did know her name. It had to be him. "Yes," Sasha answered with a nod and a quick glance. The man was no more than a shadowy profile.

They sat silent, shoulder to shoulder, watching the dance for a long moment, and then the man got up, moved to the aisle, and was quickly gone.

Kirk Harper, parked a quarter of a block away from the mouth of the alley, saw the two motorcycle officers as the lights of their heavy machines swung into the alley and headed directly for the idling van. When their brake lights flashed on, he knew George was in trouble.

George, his heart in his throat, watched the two helmeted officers in the van's rearview mirror as they climbed off their motorcycles behind the van. He had no idea what he was going to say. He wasn't even sure he could speak. What reason could he give for being in the alley in an overheated van? He knew he was going to be arrested. They had come so close. The acid-like taste of fear in his mouth began to surrender to a great feeling of failure. From inside the Shrine he heard the crowd roar. It was ten o'clock.

The two helmeted officers were walking toward the driver's side of the van when the 240-Z roared by them in second gear. The car was nothing more than a blur of noise and lights that sent up a cloud of dust and debris in its wake. The two officers went scrambling for their bikes to give chase. George breathed a sigh of relief.

Steve Tilden, parked at the far end of the alley in his VW, saw the set of headlamps roaring toward him and thought it was the van. He smiled and cranked the VW to life. When Kirk's 240-Z flashed by, he was shocked. He was even more shocked when he saw the two motorcycle officers, red lights flashing, electronic sirens whining, in pursuit. Tilden quickly turned the car off and flattened himself across the front seats. The motorcycles roared by, never slowing.

Kirk Harper drove like a wild man, roaring around corners, down alleys. He knew it would be only seconds until other police units would be joining the pursuit and it would be over. If there was a chance, it had to be now. He downshifted for a turn, glancing at his speed. The speedometer hung near seventy miles an hour. He checked his rearview mirror. The red lights of the two motorcycles were nearly a block behind. He wrenched the steering wheel to the right and braked hard. The car responded with tires screaming and smoking. Kirk made two violent right turns and then a left before he checked the rearview mirror again. It was clear. He looked ahead, picked a driveway. Braking hard, Kirk slid the 240-Z sideways and shot up the driveway and turned the lights out. Seconds later the two motorcycles flashed by, sirens screaming.

Inside the Shrine Auditorium, Sasha, along with the rest of the crowd, was on her feet applauding, watching with her heart in her throat as the stars of the ballet, Leonid and Valentina Koslov, returned for curtain call after curtain call. The applause and cheers filled the air as two, three, four curtain calls passed. Sasha bit her lip and closed her eyes in prayer.

10

The Getaway

MAJOR MARKOFF, along with KGB agent Sergei Romanovich and his four burly companions, were waiting in the west wing of the stage. After four curtain calls, Romanovich was growing impatient. When the costumed Leonid and Valentina Koslov moved to the wing and the curtains closed, Romanovich stepped forward and took them by the arms. "Come with me," he ordered.

Leonid exchanged a quick, worried look with his blonde wife. A frightened look of despair filled Valentina's face. They had been caught. And capture meant not only a return to Russia, but also certain prosecution and imprisonment. Leonid considered resistance. But there were so many men waiting, that any effort to fight them would quickly be overcome, and even if he had a chance against them, Valentina had none. He offered no resistance as Romanovich led them away from the stage. Neither bothered to speak. There was nothing to say. Leonid silently decided he would claim his wife knew nothing of the plan. It just might save her from prison.

"Wait," Major Markoff called from the edge of the curtains. The cheers and the thunder of the applause continued to come from the appreciative audience, who knew nothing of the drama going on behind the curtain. Romanovich, escorting the worried Koslovs, paused. It was as if time had stopped backstage. The costumed members of the troups knew that the presence of the Gang of Five meant trouble, and it was now obvious that the Koslovs were the focal point of it. The waiting game that had started the night before with the room restrictions was now over, and with the capture of the Koslovs, the others, at least for the time being, could breathe a sigh of relief. And they watched with a near reverent silence for the Koslovs to be ushered away. "Give them another curtain," Markoff said, not wanting to displease the crowd or stir the suspicions of the Western press with the sudden disappearance of the Koslovs.

Romanovich released Leonid and Valentina from his grip.

Leonid took Valentina's hand in his and led her back to center stage. There they posed, and the curtains parted once more. The applause and cheers increased. Leonid and Valentina bowed low.

Major Markoff waited. He knew it was the Koslovs' last bow ever, and as a Russian, his love for the ballet was as deep as any. Finally Leonid raised his head and then his body. Valentina followed his lead. A single long-stemmed rose arched through the air and landed at their feet. Valentina picked it up. The applause and cheers reached a new crescendo. Holding Valentina's hand, Leonid took a step backward. Valentina followed. The towering curtains began to slide in from the sides of the stage.

Leonid glanced to his left. Waiting were Major Markoff, Sergei Romanovich, and the others. "Do not let go of my hand," Leonid warned with a glance at his wife. Valentina managed a feeble smile, and then the curtain closed in front of them.

The startled Major Markoff and the others watched as the Koslovs bolted to their right and ran for the fire door on the east wall of the stage. It was so unexpected that valuable seconds passed before the men reacted.

Leonid put a shoulder to the door at the same instant he pushed the bar release. It sprang open into the night. "Get them!" someone shouted in Russian.

George Rollins was racing the engine of the overheated van in an effort to cool it. He knew it was going to seize and quit at any second. The engine was missing and coughing. He was leaning toward the dash to study the heat gauge, which he prayed somehow was coming down, when suddenly the side door was flung open and Leonid and Valentina dived inside.

They were in full dance costume, and the startled George just stared. Leonid Koslov shouted something in Russian but George had no idea what it was. The tall dancer, draped in a cape, slammed the door shut and locked it. A chorus of angry Russian shouts cut through the darkness, bringing George to his senses. He looked out the side window to see six men closing on the van. "Here we go!" he cried and jerked the van in gear, flooring the accelerator. The engine roared, and the van jumped forward.

A thick-necked man in a suit and tie grabbed the support bar for the van's rearview mirror and hung on as the van raced off. It was Sergei Romanovich. Sergei's angry face was only inches from George's, and he shouted commands in Russian. Leonid and Valentina clung to one another as they watched in horror. George pushed harder on the accelerator. The Russian reached through the open window at George's throat with a meaty hand. George quickly rolled the window up. Romanovich withdrew his arm and fell away as the van gained speed.

Steve Tilden cranked his VW to life as the van, lights out, roared by him. "Go, go, go!" he shouted as it flashed by. Once the van had passed, Steve pulled the VW across the mouth of the alley and shut the engine off. He didn't have to wait long. Seconds later, two sets of headlamps raced toward him. Horns blared behind the glare of the lights. Steve raised his hands, pretending problems with the car. "Sorry, she just won't go."

Angry shouts and curses filled the alley, mixing with the sound of the horns. Steve looked into the glare of the lights and shrugged. "I told you it won't go."

Car doors slammed, and four burly Russians appeared from behind the lights. They gave short, sharp commands, and grabbing the VW, they pushed it to the side of the alley. "Hey!" Steve protested. "Get your hands off my car." The Russians didn't seem threatened by his demands. The VW out of their way, they climbed into their cars and roared on.

Kirk Harper was southbound on Figueroa Street in his 240-Z when he spotted Tilden's van, spewing steam, as it raced north. He smiled, pounded the steering wheel and shouted, "Hooray!"

Kirk was making a U-turn to follow the van, when the two motorcycles appeared from a side street. They spotted him. Kirk slowed and pulled to the curb. The two motor officers pulled in behind him and stopped. He waited with his police badge and identification in hand and a sheepish look on his face when they reached him. "I can explain, guys," Kirk said just as two carloads of KGB agents roared by. The two helmeted officers exchanged a quick look and headed for their bikes. "Go get 'em, guys!" Kirk shouted.

Leonid and Valentina, in the van with George, were watching out the rear windows as the two sets of headlamps closed on them. George noticed the dancers were clinging to each other. Suddenly, behind the pursuing headlamps, red lights flashed on. The headlamps slowed, pulled to the side, and faded in the rear-view mirror. George turned, looked to the two Russians, "All right, A-OK, number one, you know?"

"Yes," Leonid Koslov smiled, "God bless America!"

"Hey, that's the spirit!" George smiled as they roared on into the night.

Kirk, in his 240-Z was the first to reach the Rollins home in Highland Park. Steve Tilden was only a few minutes behind in his VW. Both expected to see the white van parked in front of George's house. It was not.

"Where are they?" Steve demanded, climbing out of his VW.

"I don't know," Kirk answered soberly.

Both men were worried.

A long ten minutes passed, with both Steve and Kirk pacing the sidewalk before the vegetable truck turned onto the block. The two men were waiting to help Sasha down from the cab after she pulled to the curb. "Where's George?" She questioned, not seeing the van.

"He's on his way," Kirk answered, but his bluff was less than convincing.

They waited in the living room, where Kirk kept checking the window. Sasha made tea, but none of them drank it. Their fears swelled as the minutes dragged by. Sasha prayed silently. Steve and Kirk met quietly in the kitchen. "What do you think?" Steve asked. "It's almost midnight."

"I don't know," Kirk admitted.

"You think the KGB got them?" Steve questioned.

"If they did, we'll never see George again," Kirk answered softly with a glance at the doorway to the living room.

"We've got to do something," Steve urged. "Maybe we should call Lieutenant Collins."

"He'll have our heads, you know?" Kirk warned.

"You got a better idea?" Steve countered.

Eight miles away, on a dark shoulder of the northbound

Pasadena freeway, the white van sat with its rear end jacked high. The beer bottle that George ran over behind the Shrine Auditorium had finally done its work. Beside the van, the bearded George and the costumed Russian, Leonid Koslov, struggled at changing the tire. Leonid was offering advice to George in Russian.

"Hey," George complained, "I don't tell you how to dance, do I? So don't tell me how to change a tire."

The tall Russian, dressed as Prince Siegfried from Swan Lake, drew curious looks from the passing cars.

*　　*　　*

Steve and Kirk flipped a coin to see who would call the Lieutenant. Steve lost. He had the telephone in hand when George and the two Russians walked in. Cheers and shouts filled the small house. Both Sasha and Valentina were crying with joy. "Never thought I'd be glad to shake a Commie's hand," Kirk said, pumping Leonid's hand.

"Commie?" The bewildered Leonid questioned.

"Yeah," Steve explained. "It's slang for Comrade."

"Oh, Comrade," Leonid smiled.

There was no champagne, but George felt a toast was important so he returned from the kitchen with a six-pack of Coke. Cans were popped open and passed around. "Coke is it," Valentina smiled with the English she learned from Western television.

Kirk elbowed Steve, who stood beside him. "I don't wanna hurt anybody's feelings, but Russians sure wear funny shoes, don't they?"

George raised his can. The others followed his lead as they

stood in a rough circle in the living room. George with his beard, long hair, and headband, Sasha in her green satin prom dress, the two detectives in casual street clothes, and Leonid and Valentina still in full dance costume. "To freedom," George said.

"To freedom," the voices answered, and they drank.

"And thank God for America," Leonid said with a heavy accent. There were tears welling in his eyes as he raised his can a second time.

"And thank God for America," the others intoned.

11

Red Tape

THE WHITE VAN, known to the KGB, worried Tilden and Kirk, so they hid it in a small, cluttered garage behind George's house. The Russian couple, sharing a sleeping bag, spent their first night of freedom in the van. Tilden and Kirk stood guard outside. They did not sleep. They knew the KGB were highly trained agents, and there was little doubt that at least one of them had memorized the van's license number. Both men hoped they wouldn't be able to link Tilden's address in West Covina with George's home in Highland Park, but neither was sure what the KGB was capable of or to what lengths they would go in their efforts to recover two stars of the fabled Soviet Bolshoi Ballet. The reaction they witnessed at the Shrine warned them that the defection had not been taken lightly by the Soviets. The two detectives pacing in the dark dirt alley in the middle of the night were beginning to have second thoughts about the consequences of their actions.

The sound of every passing car drove Tilden and Kirk into the shadows of the alley, concealing themselves from what little light there was. Both men were carrying thirty-eights, and although they were worried about the arrival of the KGB, they were equally determined to protect the newfound freedom of the two Russian dancers.

"This is really great," Kirk complained to Tilden shortly after 2 A.M. "Here we are pulling guard duty for a couple of Commies."

"Ex-Commies," Steve corrected as he turned the collar of his jacket up against the cold.

"You think the KGB is looking for us?" Kirk questioned with a look at the mouth of the dark alley.

"Naw," Steve answered. "They're not looking for us. We're just out here because we like alleys after midnight."

"I'm serious," Kirk defended soberly.

"I think if they find us they'll try to take them back," Steve answered, equally sober. "I read somewhere that if they can lay a hand on them, they have jurisdiction over them."

"You think they've been to your place yet?" Kirk questioned as a chill made him shudder. He wasn't sure it was from the cold.

*   *   *

It was shortly after 2 A.M. when the clerk on duty at the headquarters of the Department of Motor Vehicles in Sacramento received the call. The majority of the after-hour inquiries were from law enforcement agencies whose codes took them directly into the monolithic computerized files that held information on every registered motor vehicle in the State of California, but occasionally an agency would need additional information or a file would be in transfer, which took it out of the loop, so a token crew of clerks provided the net for the multi-million-dollar system.

The senior clerk was in his third year at Berkeley, and it was there in a Foreign Affairs class that he'd met the man. It wasn't until four months later, after he'd borrowed the money to repair his Porsche, that he learned the man was an employee of the Soviet Consulate in San Francisco. He'd worried about it for a while, but the young Russian never demanded anything. As a matter of fact, he had since become a close friend who was now helping him financially through his third year. He was surprised to find it was his Russian friend on the line. "David," the Russian said in his flawless English. "I'm sorry to bother you at work, but I need some help."

"What is it?" The Berkeley student was suspicious.

"This is embarrassing," the Russian admitted over the line in a convincing tone. "But security here at the Consulate woke me up to complain about a van that's driven around the block a couple of times. You know how paranoid a Russian can be," he joked. "But with terrorism a reality we all live with, they've insisted I check it out. Personally, Dave, I think it's probably some tourist."

"Do you have a license number?" the clerk said, taking the bait.

"Sure," his Russian friend answered, "it's California license eight-five-three-F-W-V."

It seemed logical. Harmless. He was asking for information anyone could buy from any branch of the Department of Motor Vehicles during regular business hours. It was public information. He knew it was a violation of the Department's policy to give the information to unauthorized sources over the telephone, but everyone did it, and he owed the Russian a favor. What could it hurt?

"Just a minute," he said to his Russian friend as he punched the information into a computer keyboard in front of him. A second later the information appeared in soft green letters on the computer's video screen.

```
        MON   9/17/79          0214A      DMV/SAC

  INQ  CA      853FWV
  FILE CA      853 FWV


  FORD VAN ECON '76
  VIN   2R11X11697
  REG/0       TILDEN, STEVEN S.
  2107 SAINT ELMO DR., WEST COVINA, CA.
  LEG/O - SAME


  REG/X      3/12/80
  DATE/ISS   6/23/78
  DATE F/S   4/11/76


  END                          CR6-D
                               DMV/SAC
```

Twenty minutes later and nearly four hundred miles to the south, a rented sedan turned onto Saint Elmo Drive in West Covina. The block was dark and quiet. The beige Ford parked a few doors from 2107 and switched its lights off.

At the University Hilton in South Los Angeles, Major Markoff placed a voice-scrambling device over the receiver of the telephone in his hotel room and dialed the number he had memorized when he was in Moscow. He listened to the telephone ring three, four, five times before finally a female voice answered, "What number are you calling?"

Markoff recognized the voice. "I'm calling for Tom," he answered.

"I'm sorry, Tom isn't here anymore," the female answered in his ear.

"Did he move back to his beach house?" the Major questioned as part of the code.

"This had better be important," the voice warned, satisfied with his authentication.

"I have a telephone listed in West Covina that's been making multi-unit message calls to Monterey Heights. I need to know the name in Monterey Heights, and I need to know if there have been any calls from there to Northeast Los Angeles."

"You're looking for Sasha?"

The Major didn't answer the question. "When can I have the information?"

"It's the middle of the night, you know?"

"We must leave for the airport at nine. I don't have much time."

"All right, what's the number?"

"Two-seven-six, eight-one-four-oh," Markoff answered.

"I'll call you back," the sultry voice promised and hung up.

*   *   *

The FBI Command Post was deactivated two hours after the curtain closed on the final performance at the Shrine Auditorium, but the flurry of activity by the KGB had the lights on at FBI headquarters in West Los Angeles. Harmon Marshal sat with George Wills in his office while the duty officer offered the latest intelligence briefing.

"We've talked with LAPD intelligence, and they advise that at 22:04 this date a team of motor officers stopped two Hertz rental cars, a blue '79 Ford LTD and a green '79 Ford Fairlane that were observed speeding northbound on Figueroa Street just north of

Adams Boulevard." The young FBI officer paused to adjust his horn-rim glasses and glance at Harmon and George Wills. When there were no questions, he continued. "The blue LTD was driven by Sergei Romanovich, known KGB. In his company were Nikolai Rozhko and Yuri Vanagel, also confirmed KGB. In the green Fairlane were Ivan Barsukov and Vikor Lisovsky, also both KGB."

"Where were they going?" Harmon Marshal wondered aloud.

"The report doesn't say," the duty officer answered dryly.

"What does it say?" George Wills pressed.

"It says the drivers of both vehicles were cited for exceeding the posted speed limit and ordered to appear at the municipal traffic court on South Wall Street within ten days."

"You can bet they'll both be there," George Wills teased.

"Thank you, Cannon," Harmon Marshal said, dismissing the duty officer.

"You're welcome, sir," he said and moved for the door, closing it behind him.

Harmon rocked back in his cushioned chair and looked to George Wills. "Well, George, any ideas?"

George ran a hand back over his thinning, gray hair. "I just can't figure it. From the activity we observed, it looks like they were pursuing someone, but no one saw anything, and the Soviets haven't reported anyone missing."

"Everything still quiet at the hotel?" Harmon questioned.

"Looks like business as usual in preparation for their flight to Moscow in the morning."

Harmon glanced at his watch. "If someone had defected, we should have heard something from them by now."

"If someone pulled off a defection there tonight, with the security the Soviets had, and the men we had, and got away with it, it could only be one group."

"The CIA!"

"Who else?"

*   *   *

"George?" Sasha whispered in the quiet darkness of their bedroom. She wasn't sure her husband was awake.

"Yeah," George answered, turning a shoulder to Sasha. They were but shadowy profiles in the bedroom's dim light.

"I'm really proud of you," Sasha said, moving her head to his shoulder. George slid an arm around his wife and drew her closer to him. "You're the one who had to go into the lion's den," George answered, "not me."

It was quiet for a moment, and then Sasha spoke again. "Did you see their faces, George? Weren't they happy?"

"Kinda made it all worthwhile, didn't it?" George answered.

*   *   *

It was nearly 3 A.M., and Major Vladimir Markoff knew that time was running out. He stood near the window of his hotel room with the curtains open, looking out over the night lights of South Los Angeles. Tomorrow night, he told himself, he would be able to stand at the window of his apartment in Moscow and look out over the lights. Searching the pinpoints of light that spread in all directions before him, he wondered what lay ahead. There was little doubt that Colonel Kirsanov would hold him personally responsible for the defection. He had run the events of the evening through his mind a thousand times preparing his report. The only area he felt vulnerable about was his failure to cover Sasha. Had he ordered her followed, they would know where the Koslovs were, but in their overconfidence, they ignored her as nothing more than a frightened woman who posed no possible threat, and in the confusion that followed, she simply vanished into the night. Markoff still felt he was no more responsible than the Colonel was, but rank did afford one the right to accuse, and many times the right to condemn. The telephone rang. Markoff turned and looked at it. Had they found Sasha? Did he still have time to organize a capture attempt? Could they get away from the hotel undetected? A rush of thoughts flooded his mind as he moved to pick up the receiver. "Hello," he said in English.

"I'll be brief," the familiar female voice said in his ear. "The individuals you're interested in are police officers. That makes it too risky — I'm sorry." It sounded sincere. "I must go," she added and hung up. The dial tone hummed in Markoff's ear. He lowered the receiver and hung up.

*　　*　　*

Sasha was up early. Like everyone else, she had not slept. She was busy fixing breakfast when Valentina entered the small kitchen wearing a blouse and jeans Sasha had given her the night before. "Good morning," Valentina smiled in Russian.

"Good morning," Sasha answered, pouring her a cup of coffee.

Valentina was sitting down at the table when she spotted the small cross on the kitchen wall. "You are a Christian?" she questioned cautiously as Sasha set the cup of coffee in front of her.

"Yes," Sasha smiled, "and in America we don't have to whisper about it."

*　　*　　*

Steve and Kirk were in the living room with George and Leonid. Leonid no longer looked like Prince Siegfried from Swan Lake. He was wearing a plaid shirt and jeans that George had loaned him. They had listened to the radio news earlier and were surprised when there was no mention of the defection. Now they were gathered around the small color television set in the living room, switching from channel to channel in search of news. Again there was no mention of the defection. "I don't get it," Kirk complained as George shut off the television. "Those Commies were as mad as hornets. I can't believe it didn't even make the local news."

"Maybe it's not news because the Russians don't want anyone to know about it," Steve suggested soberly.

"Why wouldn't they want anyone to know about it?" George questioned.

"Would you? If you were still looking for them?" Steve added.

It was a sobering thought, and although Leonid did not understand the words, he knew from the faces that it was a serious discussion. Kirk caught Leonid's dark eyes and read the worry they couldn't hide. Kirk patted Leonid on the knee. "Don't worry, Leonard," he winked, "we won't let those Commies get you back."

"I think it's time we get some help," Steve suggested.

"What's your idea?" Kirk probed.

"Let's start with the FBI," Steve answered.

George picked up the telephone and handed it to Steve. "Thanks," Steve said with a burning look at George.

"Good morning, Federal Bureau of Investigation. May I help you?" the pleasant female voice said into Steve's ear.

"I hope so. I'd like to talk to someone about a defection."

"A defection, sir?" The woman sounded puzzled. "You mean you have something that won't work?"

"No, I mean, to defect."

"Oh, a political defection. I see. Where do you plan to defect to, Sir?"

"It's not me. I'm an American. It's a — friend."

"I see. You have a friend that plans to defect."

"No, he already has."

"And you're trying to get in touch with him?"

"No, listen to me. I just need some information about defections. May I speak to an agent please?"

"Sir, defections are usually not under the jurisdiction of the Bureau. The primary purpose of the FBI is the enforcement of federal law within the domestic United States."

"May I speak to an agent, please?" Steve repeated slowly in an effort to control his growing anger with the woman.

"Sir, the Los Angeles office of the Federal Bureau of Investigation receives hundreds of calls every day and it's my responsibility to screen them in an attempt to save both you and the Bureau valuable time."

Steve took in a breath to calm himself. "I have in my company a citizen of a Communist country who would like to defect to the United States. Do you understand that?"

"Yes."

"I need some advice on procedure," Steve continued. "May I talk to an agent?"

"Please hold," the female voice said, and the sound of music drifted over the line. Steve shook his head and looked at the waiting trio of faces. "Did you know the FBI plays elevator music?"

"They put you on hold?" George questioned.

The switchboard operator at the Federal Building rang the duty officer's desk while she kept Steve's call on hold.

"This is Parker," the duty officer said, picking up his telephone.

"Agent Parker, this is Karen on the board. I have a male caller on line six who insists on talking to an agent."

The tone in the operator's voice told the agent the caller was a nuisance call, but Bureau policy dictated that those who insisted on talking to an agent be given the opportunity. "What's he want?" Agent Parker questioned.

"I'm not sure," the operator answered. "He keeps changing his story. Something about a defection."

"Probably another irate taxpayer calling to announce he's defecting to Australia," Parker chuckled. "We've had three this month."

"Shall I put him through?"

"Yeah, I'll handle it."

The music on the line ended as a voice said, "This is Special Agent Parker. May I help you?"

"Yes," Steve answered, signaling to the others to be quiet. "I need some information on defection procedures."

"The FBI doesn't handle defections, sir. You'll have to call the INS."

"I know that, but this one is unique, a little sensitive," Steve defended.

"I'm sure it is, sir, but we can't help you. Call the INS." The agent hung up abruptly.

"He hung up on me!" Steve said in disbelief.

"He what?" Kirk questioned.

"He said call the INS and hung up," Steve repeated.

"Now you know where all the dropouts from the police academy go," Kirk growled as he reached to take the telephone from Steve.

"Why would they hang up on you?" George said to Steve.

"I guess they've got more important things than freedom to worry about," Steve answered.

Kirk got the telephone number for the Immigration and Naturalization Service, the INS, from information and dialed it. He was determined to get results.

"When this is over," Steve warned, now angry, "I'm going to the FBI office and introduce myself to Agent Parker. We're going to have a nice little heart-to-heart talk about public service."

"Don't let it bother you," George urged.

Kirk quieted them with a wave of the hand as the telephone rang in his ear.

"Good morning, INS," a female voice answered.

"Yes, I'd like to report two people who have made an illegal entry into the United States," Kirk said with a smug look at George and Steve.

"I'll transfer you to our Enforcement Division. Hold on please."

"Good morning, Passports. May I help you?"

"The lady said she was transferring me to Enforcement," Kirk complained.

"I'm sorry, this is Passports."

"Can you transfer me?"

"Who were you calling?"

"Enforcement."

"Hold, please."

Kirk waited.

"I'm sorry, sir. That line's busy, could you call back?"

Kirk hung up.

Kirk called back three times before getting through to the Enforcement Division. An agent listened to the story of the defection without comment, then answered, "INS can help you, but I don't think this is an Enforcement problem. Let me transfer you to the Director's office."

"Mr. Sewell's office."

"Yes, Detective Kirk Harper, Los Angeles Police calling."

"I'm sorry, Detective, Mr. Sewell is in the field this morning. Can I take a message?"

"Does he have an assistant?" Kirk questioned impatiently.

"That would be Mr. Bendici."

"May I talk to him?"

"He's in the field with Mr. Sewell. If you could call back after ten."

Kirk hung up. He was redfaced with frustration. "I wonder if Alexander Graham Bell knew what he was getting us into?" he said with a look at others.

"This Alex Bell?" Leonid questioned in thick halting English, "he will help us?"

"We hope so," George smiled.

* * *

Steve Tilden glanced at his watch, then to Kirk. "If we'd left ten minutes ago, we still would have been late for work."

Kirk nodded agreement, looked to George and Leonid. "We," he said talking loud and tapping himself on the chest. "He and I," he pointed to Steve, "have to go to work." He gestured with walking fingers.

"Kirk," George interrupted.

"Yeah."

"I understand English."

"Yeah, OK," Kirk answered. "I was just trying to let Leonard know what was happening."

Steve stood up. "Just sit tight, George," he recommended. "Keep everybody inside. Don't answer the door unless it's Kirk or me."

"We'll call as soon as we can get a few answers," Kirk added.

Leonid saw the two men were about to leave so he stood and offered his hand to Kirk. "Thank you," he said in accented English.

"Piece of cake," Kirk smiled, shaking his hand.

"Piece of cake," Leonid smiled at Steve, offering his hand.

12

Show and Tell

LIEUTENANT JACK COLLINS, or Jack the Ripper, as Kirk called
him, was sitting at his desk in the Detective Bureau of the
Wilshire Division police station when detectives Kirk Harper
and Steve Tilden walked into the squad room. The Lieutenant
casually checked his watch. The two men were forty minutes late.
He waited until they had sat down at their desks before he pushed
away from his.

The Lieutenant was a sober, humorless man who considered
police service a profession that required dedication, devotion,
and sacrifice—none of which he had been able to find in
Detectives Tilden and Harper. He noticed neither man had
shaved.

"Morning, Jack," Kirk smiled when Collins reached their desk.
He knew the Lieutenant did not like being addressed by his first
name.

"What's the excuse this week?" the Lieutenant questioned as
he burned a look at the two men. "Last Monday you were late
because a meteorite hit your fishing boat and sank it off Long
Beach. The week before that, your car keys were lost in a flash

151

flood in the desert. I can hardly wait to hear what it is this week."

Tilden and Harper exchanged a look. They agreed silently that Tilden would explain. Tilden looked at the Lieutenant. "You're not going to believe this, Lieutenant."

"You're right," Lieutenant Collins agreed, "but try me anyway."

"We helped two Russian Bolshoi dancers defect last night," Steve Tilden said proudly.

Lieutenant Collins' face clouded with anger. The two detectives could see it. "You two would use anything as an excuse, wouldn't you?"

"But, Lieutenant—" Steve pleaded.

"This is no time for your stupid jokes, Tilden," the Lieutenant growled. "Kidnapping those two dancers could cause the LAPD international embarrassment."

Steve and Kirk exchanged a look of surprise. "Kidnapping?"

"That's right," the lieutenant continued. "They were kidnapped from the Shrine Auditorium last night. Half the department's out looking for them."

"Lieutenant," Kirk warned, "if you wanna collect your pension, you'd better sit down and listen."

*　　*　　*

Forty minutes after Lieutenant Collins listened to the story Kirk and Steve told, the Detective Bureau was crowded with twelve FBI Agents, four Secret Service men, eight officials from the Immigration and Naturalization Service, six Federal Marshals, a senior State Department aide who had been passing through Los Angeles on his way to Japan, the Chief of Police, and a wealth of LAPD brass.

Kirk and Steve were promptly separated and ordered by the FBI to tell where the two Russians were being held.

"Either of you guys Special Agent Parker?" Tilden questioned the two men with him.

"They're not being held anywhere," Harper told the two agents questioning him.

"You've made this whole thing up?"

"No, I just mean they're not being held. They're free. Like I used to be."

Neither man would talk. The chief of police was livid. After a fruitless and frustrating thirty minutes, he ordered both men moved into the Division Commander's office. Kirk was already there when Steve was escorted in. When the door was closed and they were alone, Kirk looked at Steve. "Did they offer you any coffee?"

"No," Steve answered.

"I noticed all the brass had coffee."

"In the movies they always give the guy being questioned a cup of coffee," Steve complained.

"Probably low budget," Kirk suggested. Then he added, "Did you tell them anything?"

Steve shook his head. "Naw, I thought I'd leave that to you."

"I told last time."

"No, I'm pretty sure I did."

"Nope, I did. It's your turn."

In the crowded tape room where the conversation was being monitored and recorded, Lieutenant Collins looked to Captain Meeker. "They know we're listening. I know them. They're toying with us."

*　　*　　*

Lieutenant Collins was carrying two cups of coffee when he stepped into the Commander's office, where Steve and Kirk sat waiting. "Thought you guys might like a cup," Collins said with a forced smile.

"Why, Lieutenant," Kirk smiled, "how thoughtful of you."

"Listen, fellas," Collins pleaded, sitting down with the two. "You've really put me in a tough spot."

"How's that, Jack, ol' buddy?" Kirk needled.

"This refusing to tell where the Russians are," the Lieutenant explained. "It's causing us a lot of embarrassment."

"We never meant to embarrass anyone," Steve defended. "We just don't want that army of feds out there descending on our friend's house."

"How about this, Jack," Kirk suggested, slapping the Lieutenant on the shoulder. "What if I call them and have them come to the station?"

"You're serious?" the Lieutenant questioned cautiously.

"Very," Steve assured.

Lieutenant Collins moved for the door. "I'll be right back."

The irate collection of officials argued and debated for five minutes before they finally reached agreement on a choice that really wasn't theirs in the first place.

"All right, Lieutenant," Harmon Marshal from the FBI said, acting as the spokesman, "have them make the call."

"Hello," George Rollins answered as he picked up the telephone in the kitchen.

"George, it's Kirk."

"How's it going?" George questioned.

"Pretty good. Listen, do you think you could drive our two friends down here to the station?"

"Sure," George answered. "You're on West Pico, right?"

"Yeah, just west of Sears."

"Be there in thirty minutes."

The call was recorded as well as traced by the FBI.

*   *   *

The six Federal Marshals were posted and waiting near the entrance to the station's parking lot. They were watching for the arrival of George and the two Russians, but they ignored the faded flatbed truck when it pulled to the curb in front. Nor did they notice the bearded George along with Leonid in his plaid shirt and the blond Valentina in her faded jeans as they walked to the front entrance of the police station.

There was a broad-shouldered, handsome, thirty-year-old black officer behind the reception desk. He offered a wide white smile of recognition to Leonid as they reached him. "Hey, what's happening?"

As soon as the man spoke, Leonid remembered him from his morning jog a few days earlier. "What's happening?" Leonid smiled in response.

"You two know each other?" the surprised George questioned.

"We've done a little runnin' together," the black officer smiled. "Now, what can I do for you?"

"Detective Harper is expecting us," George answered.

"Harper!" the black officer said. "Hey is this—are these the two Russians?"

155

"Yes," Leonid beamed. "Bolshoi."

"Right, Bolshoi."

After being ushered into the heart of the station, George, Leonid, and Valentina, like Kirk and Steve, were promptly separated and the horde of Federal officials and agents began an interrogation that was to last for over three hours.

The two FBI agents with Leonid spoke fluent Russian, and at first it frightened the wary and suspicious Soviets. The years of deceit and paranoia were not easily discarded, and to Leonid the two men were strangers, and perhaps even KGB. To ease Leonid's fears, the two agents brought in Kirk. Although he understood little, if any, that was said, he offered Leonid the security he needed.

"Go ahead, Leonard," Kirk said, sitting down beside Leonid. "Tell 'em whatever you want. They're on our side."

The two FBI agents were skilled interrogators, and their early questions were designed to establish an important rapport. The youngest of the two spoke of his several visits to the Soviet Union. He had even once attended a Bolshoi performance in Moscow. Once Leonid relaxed, the questions turned more serious. Was Leonid a member of the Communist Party? Did he have any family members in the Soviet Armed Forces? Had he ever worked for the GRU or the KGB? Did he know how many KGB traveled with the troupe? Did he know their names? Who was the senior KGB officer?

Leonid was candid and cooperative until the questions turned to the planning of the defection.

"Someone in the troupe helped you with your plans to defect?"

"Da," Leonid nodded.

"Obviously he is a friend?"

"Yes, he is a friend," Leonid agreed.

"And he returned to Moscow?"

"Yes, he returned."

"Why?"

"He felt he had to," Leonid answered sincerely.

"Who is this man?"

"I cannot tell you his name."

"You can trust us," the agent assured.

"I gave him my word," Leonid defended. "He knows his life is in my hands — and it is safe there."

"Don't you think the KGB will find him?" the agent pressed. "We might be able to help."

"No," Leonid answered confidently. "The KGB will not discover him."

*   *   *

After the interviews were over, Harmon Marshal from the FBI and William Alan, the aide from the State Department, met in the privacy of the Detective Commander's office.

"What does the Bureau know of these two?" William Alan asked Marshal as he sat down behind the Captain's desk and lit a cigarette.

"Nothing dramatic," Harmon Marshal answered. "Leonid was a member of the Young Communist League and sort of the political ramrod for the troupe, but it seems he was only using that for career advantages."

"And Valentina?"

"Basically non-political."

"And you see no reason to oppose their asylum?"

"None."

"All right, I'll call the Secretary. The basis for their request will be a desire for religious freedom, since both profess to be Christian. There is little doubt the request will be granted."

"Bill, before you call Washington," Harmon Marshal said, "let's talk about how this defection occurred."

"You mean the official version," Alan questioned.

"I mean on the surface this looks like it could cause some professional embarrassment," Harmon suggested tactfully. "You and I know that these people, although well intended, are rank amateurs. Sheer blind luck got them through this thing."

"George Rollins told me they had God on their side," Alan smiled.

"I think it's important a certain image be maintained, not only for the sake of the Bureau's morale, but also for our relations with the KGB as well as the Soviet government. If they think this got out of our hands it could hurt future operations."

Alan drew on his cigarette. "I see your point." He exhaled smoke toward the ceiling as he considered the suggestion. "We could put an 'Interest of National Security' blanket on it."

"That would be greatly appreciated," Harmon assured.

"None of the principals seem that interested in talking to the press. You could suggest that it would serve to protect the contact who returned to the Soviet Union."

"I think they already know that."

"All right, Harmon, you've got a deal. But, you owe me one."

*   *   *

A conference was held with the LAPD and INS, and it was decided that in the best interest of all concerned, the real story of the defection would be kept confidential.

The State Department, as well as the FBI, offered to host the defectors while their application for political asylum was processed. The two Russians conferred briefly, and then the usually quiet Valentina Koslova announced they felt safer with George Rollins. "We are believers in Jesus Christ — like George," Valentina declared.

13

The Final Note

TUESDAY MORNING A MEETING was held in the Federal Building in downtown Los Angeles. Present were Leonid Koslov and his wife, Valentina, as well as several high-ranking Soviet diplomats from the Soviet Consulate in San Francisco.

They met in a fourth floor conference room. Harmon Marshal from the FBI, as well as the young FBI agent who spoke Russian and the local Director of the Immigration and Naturalization Service, were with them.

"They will immediately try to establish an intimate psychological contact with both of you," the young FBI agent warned Leonid and Valentina before they stepped through the door into the conference room. "Remember, they will want you to feel lost, confused. They'll offer to take you home."

"We are home," Leonid answered confidently, and they stepped through the door.

A KGB officer, a handsome, dark-haired man in a dark suit, posing as a Deputy from the Soviet Consulate in San Francisco, stood to his feet as Leonid and Valentina entered the room. "My dear friends," he said in Russian. "It is such a relief to see you. Are you all right?"

Leonid and Valentina sat down at the long, polished table. Two other Soviets, a sober woman with blue-gray hair and a chunky man sat at the other end of the table.

Valentina clung to her husband's arm and refused more than a glance at them.

"We are fine," Leonid assured the man, as he sat rigid in his chair.

The handsome Russian moved closer to them, studying their faces. Valentina averted her eyes. Leonid challenged the man with a bold look of determination.

"I am an official of the Soviet Consulate in San Francisco," the Russian began, "and I want to tell you how worried your comrades with the Bolshoi are about you. They, along with the Soviet government, know that what has happened is not your fault."

"What has happened to us is of our own choice," Leonid answered.

"Leonid," the handsome Russian pleaded softly, leaning on the table, "please listen to me. You are a magnificent, gifted artist. You and your lovely wife, Valentina, are the pride of the Motherland. We cherish you. You are Bolshoi. I am here to take you home. I know there is a simple explanation for what has happened, and I can assure you on the highest authority that it is forgiven. We don't even want an explanation.

"Your families, your friends, most don't even know anything has happened. So little time has passed. There won't even be any excuses to make."

Leonid and Valentina exchanged a look, and pushed from their chairs. The handsome KGB officer offered a warm smile and an open extended hand. "Come home, come with me."

"No," Leonid said to the Soviet. "We are staying. I may become a driver of vegetable trucks—here even they believe as they choose."

* * *

George and Sasha waited in a rear office along with Detectives Kirk Harper and Steve Tilden. It was a long, agonizing wait. They all knew the pressure the Soviets could, and would, apply.

Kirk was pacing the room. "I don't see why they had to talk to these Commies anyway."

"They didn't have to," George explained. "They did it because they wanted to."

"That makes it even more stupid," Kirk shot back at George.

"I think it's important to Leonid and Valentina," Steve Tilden defended.

"Remember," Kirk said, pausing to look first at Steve and then to George and Sasha. "He's the one who thought the two people from Fort Wayne were Russians."

"Why do you think it's important to them, Steve?" Sasha questioned.

"Because they had to run," Steve explained. "At the Shrine, surrounded by the KGB, Leonid and Valentina had no choice. Now they don't have to run. I think it's important for them to face the Soviets, and show them they're not afraid, and perhaps even more important, to show them why."

The door opened, and Leonid and Valentina stepped in. They were smiling. Leonid raised his hands in victory. The room was filled with shouts and cheers and tears.

Leonid spoke in his broken English. "I pledge allegiance— God bless America!"

14

Meet the Press

TUESDAY MORNING THE HEADLINES of the Los Angeles Times read, *"TWO MORE RUSSIAN DANCERS DEFECT."* It was news not only in Los Angeles, not only in the United States, but everywhere in the free world. The State Department, although hounded for details, released only a brief, terse statement that gave few details of the defection. The press smelled a story, and the determined ferrets went to work.

George and Sasha continued to host their newfound Russian friends while Detectives Steve Tilden and Kirk Harper returned to investigating crime in the city of the Angels. None of them sought, or wanted, the limelight, although they were American heroes in the truest sense.

Wednesday morning a segment producer from the CBS news program "60 Minutes" knocked on George's door. He, like the producer from ABC's "20/20" that preceded him, went away empty-handed. The National Enquirer, Newsweek, and People magazine rounded out the morning. Sasha turned them all away. The Russian couple were no longer in her home and she wasn't interested in talking to anyone.

It was true. The Russian couple were no longer in the Rollins' home. At least not for the moment. Being disciplined Bolshoi, Leonid and Valentina needed to exercise and work out, and perhaps most important, they needed to dance. The principal of the Acadia Junior High School, four blocks from the Rollins home, was a deacon in George's church, and he was pleased to turn the school's gymnasium into a dance studio for the needed two-hour workout. Several teachers, a black custodian, a school bus driver, and George Rollins were the audience for the first American performance of Leonid and Valentina Koslov.

*　　*　　*

It was late in the day, and Detective Steve Tilden was locking up his desk when the telephone rang. "Wilshire Detectives, Tilden speaking," he said, gathering up the receiver.

"Yes, Detective Tilden," a female voice purred in his ear. "I'm Bonnie Simmons. I'm the talent coordinator for "The Merv Griffin Show," and we'd love to have you on our show tonight."

"Tonight?" Steve questioned.

"Yes," the voice went on. "I could have a limo pick you up at your home. We'd be glad to share dinner with you. Our other guests tonight are Charro and Kenny Rogers."

"Kenny Rogers!" Steve said. He was impressed. "Maybe I could bring my banjo and play a little backup."

The line was quiet a minute. Then the woman questioned cautiously. "You're kidding, aren't you?"

"You mean that's not why you're calling?" Steve said in mock surprise.

"I'm calling because of your involvement in the recent defection."

"I'm sorry," Steve said. "I never discuss defections on the first date." He hung up and headed for the door.

*　　*　　*

Kirk Harper's excited wife was on the telephone when he arrived home. "Kirk," she called, cupping the receiver with a hand. "It's Time Magazine. They want to know if you have a moment to talk."

"Sorry, dear," Kirk answered sarcastically as he walked through the room. "Tell them I'm on my way to Africa to fight a famine."

*　　*　　*

Early Thursday morning while the city still slept, George Rollins started his flatbed truck and backed it into the street. A wealthy Russian immigrant in Washington, D.C., had sent airline tickets for Leonid and Valentina. He was willing to help with the rebuilding of their careers in the West. They were leaving on an early flight from the Los Angeles airport.

Sasha said her goodbyes at the door. There were hugs and tears and emotion-filled words that could never capture what they felt, and then they were gone.

At the airport George pulled the big flatbed truck to the curb in front of the United Airlines terminal. He helped the blonde Valentina down from the cab while Leonid unloaded the bags from the flatbed.

"Well," George said, extending a hand to Leonid. Leonid ignored the hand and stepped to George and first hugged him and then kissed him. "Good bye, George," Leonid said. Then Valentina kissed him. "May God bless," she whispered as a tear spilled down her cheek.

George stood and watched until the two disappeared into the sea of faces inside the terminal, and then he turned to his waiting truck.

The big silver DC-10 was at 6,000 feet when it turned back over the city of Los Angeles for its non-stop flight to Washington, D.C. The freeways below, packed with their usual bumper-to-bumper morning traffic, were mere laces of concrete woven across the urban sprawl. The two faces were pressed close to the window and although they'd flown many times before, they were looking at the country below for the first time as their own. They could not see the faded flatbed truck that was northbound on the Harbor Freeway—but God could.

THE END

Author's Note

The story you have just read is true. Only certain names and locations have been changed to protect privacy and, in some instances, lives. George and Sasha Rollins, as well as Detectives Kirk Harper and Steve Tilden, did not seek, nor do they want, the limelight, although I think you will agree they are American heroes in the truest sense of the word.

While I served as a Los Angeles police officer, I worked as a partner with Detective Steve Tilden. It was through Steve that I learned of the defection only hours after it occurred.

As friends, my wife and I were present in George Rollins' home the morning after the defection. It was thrilling to learn of the story and to meet Leonid and Valentina.

Freedom has a price. America has known how high that price can be from the time of its birth until today, yet the valor of a few has paid the price for many, and I, like so many of us, am quick to forget that the freedom I wake up to daily did not always exist and without vigilance it will not always remain.

The principles of God's word guided the decisions on which America has built its foundation and history. Our forefathers have given eloquent testimony to that fact. President Lincoln once said, "It is the duty of nations, as well as men, to owe their dependence upon the over ruling power of God, and to recognize the sublime truth announced in the Holy Scriptures and proven by all history that those nations only are blessed whose God is the Lord."

Ben Franklin declared, "The longer I live, the more convincing proofs I see of the truth that God governs in the affairs of men, and if a sparrow cannot fall to the ground without His notice, is it probable that an empire can arise without His aid? We have been assured in the Sacred Writings that 'except the Lord build the house, they labor in vain that build it."

And America's house was built—and upon her walls Americans proudly proclaimed that God had built it.

On the dome of the Nation's Capitol in Washington, D.C., these words appear, "The New Testament according to the Lord and Savior, Jesus Christ." And in the House and Senate these words appear, "In God We Trust."

The Ten Commandments hang over the head of the Chief Justice of the United States Supreme Court, and the Great Seal of the United States is inscribed with a phrase, "*annuit coeptis*," which means, "God has smiled on our undertaking."

These aren't just signs hung on walls. These convictions are a part of America itself. It's not the buildings, the memorials, or the monuments that make the words great, but rather the fact that Americans believe they are true.

George Rollins knows they are true, and now so do Leonid and Valentina Koslov. Wherever they are, they breathe free, and so shall it remain as long as we all raise our hands as Leonid did and declare, "I pledge allegiance..."